FALLING FOR MY NEMESIS

A Novel

Tia Souders

JOIN MY VIP READERS CLUB!

Discover deals on my books, giveaways, new releases, and more!

Go to my site at tiasouders.com and click on the *Subscribe* tab.

WELCOME

Welcome to the town of Sweet Water, NC.

1 Town. 1 School. 12 Sweet Romances.

CHAPTER ONE

My life was a wreck, and this was my current state of chaos.

I glanced around the gymnasium at my fellow classmates as I pulled my strawberry-blonde hair up into a messy bun. It was hard to be invested in any class when it felt like your life was crumbling around your feet. As if this period weren't useless enough, there was a sub today, which meant gym was pretty much a free-for-all. Mr. Gorby, a frequent sub at Sweet Water, was notorious for maintaining a consistent lack of control in the classroom.

The boys were currently playing a rather barbaric game of basketball—grunting and shoving, checking other guys into the ground. Meanwhile, a smattering of girls did their hair on the bleachers while the rest of us walked laps around the gym, pretending to "exercise" when really most of us were just gossiping and ogling the boys on the skins team. Myself included.

And don't forget to add the pleasurable bouquet emanating from the cafeteria across the hall to the ambiance. I mean, who doesn't like the smell of sweat and hot dogs? Am I right?

Still, that didn't deter me from making my assessment as I strolled beside Harper and she chattered on about the Snowflake Ball, to which I had yet to snag a date.

I allowed my gaze to drift over the boys—my prospects—mentally checking off the roster in my head. Lucas Addington—taken. (Besides, I preferred jocks.) Ky Andrews—double taken. Wes Schultz. . .my gaze took an extra second to ponder his physique. He had the dark hair blue-eyed thing going for him, which I loved, but Lauren Carmichael snatched him up earlier in the year when they ended their family feud. *Dang.*

Who else. . .? My gaze drifted right over Jett. Harper's presence beside me served as a reminder that he, too, was unavailable. *That left...*

I made a final round with my gaze and paused when my eyes zeroed in on Carson Brooks, then I groaned. Not him. Anyone but him.

"Mia, *hello*?" Harper snapped her fingers in front of my face. "I asked you a question."

"Oh," I tore my gaze away from Carson, grateful for the distraction. The last thing I wanted was for him to catch me staring. He might think I liked the view, which I most certainly did not. "What'd you ask me?"

"Still no date yet, to the Snowflake Ball?" Harper asked, blinking down at me.

"Nope. But I have more important things to worry about, like the fact that I have yet to hear back about early admissions at any of the schools I applied to." Or the fact that my parents were on the verge of divorce. My family was falling apart, and I was helpless to stop it—just another cherry on top of the rapidly melting sundae that was my life.

Harper scrunched her nose and tucked a lock of brown hair behind her ear. "Early admissions? I didn't realize you applied for any of those."

I grunted. Harper was great, but right now, I really needed my best friend, Ethan. He'd understand that when I said I'm worried about college admissions, what I really meant was I needed some good news—something, anything to lift the mood at home, which was currently set to epic levels of despair. My parents were fighting on the daily, turning what started as little spats into brutal screaming matches, and if I could just get some news worth celebrating, maybe I could bring us together again. Maybe I could stop the war. Worst-case scenario, an acceptance letter meant I had an escape come fall.

The fight from this morning flashed in my head. The one I overheard on my way out the door. My mother had gone on one of her shopping sprees again, and Dad was not happy about it. Though I had no idea why. My family had plenty of money. Maybe we weren't rich like the Schultzes or the Carmichaels, but we did well. Who cared if Mom blew a few hundred on crap she didn't need? At least she wasn't drooling over her new assistant at work. Or, at least that's what Mom accused him of the other night during one of our fun-filled family dinners.

"Yeah. They start letting people know this month," I said, returning to the present.

Harper's brow furrowed. "Where'd you apply again?"

"A couple different places, but Duke is my first pick."

"Nice. Close enough to home but far enough away you have an excuse to stay on campus."

Yeah. Maybe two hours, too close.

I snorted. "Tell that to Ethan. He'd rather I just go to the community college here."

"Well, you two have been attached at the hip since the Brooks moved here in grade school."

My lips quirked. "True."

"So, if you don't have a date to the Snow-flake Ball, why don't you and Ethan go together?"

I wish. "He's already taking someone."

Out of all my friends, I was the only loser without a date. How fun. Normally, Ethan was my back-up, but not this time, which kind of stunk because friends were the best dates at dances, any-way. Not that I had much to compare to. I hadn't dated anyone since my sophomore year when Greg Harlow dumped me because he said I was a prude, the jerk. It wasn't my fault I have a moral compass and he was disgusting.

Since then, I forgot all about finding a love life. I'd been too busy trying to please my par-ents, be the perfect daughter, the ideal student to so much as flirt with another boy. I was barely hanging onto my family as it was. I was the glue—neutral ground. I may as well call myself Switzer-land. And if I could just hang in there a few more months, then I'd be off to school, and if they fell apart, at least I could say I tried. At least I wouldn't have a front-row seat.

I sighed as I looked at Harper's sorrowful ex-pression, and she said, "You could always just go stag?"

I groaned. Yeah, I could. If I wanted to commit social suicide.

A burst of laughter from center-court stole my attention. I glanced over to see Carson cackling with Olivia, a basketball casually hooked under his arm, looking as carefree as ever.

I rolled my eyes and turned back to Harper. Typical. Of course he would be fawning all over someone like her. He was probably going to the dance with either her or Tasha, one of Sweet Water's MG's. They might be popular and beautiful, but they earned their nickname as the school's Mean Girls for a reason. I couldn't imagine if I showed up dateless. No doubt Carson would relish the opportunity to rub my solo-status in my face.

I could picture it now, those crystal blue eyes glittering menacingly under the disco ball in the gym, his hair dark and rumpled. *Couldn't get a date, Shorty?* he'd say, and then I'd punch him.

Ugh. Why was I even thinking about him?

I crossed my arms over my chest and mustered a smile. "No worries. I'm sure I'll—"

My words cut off at the sound of someone yelling, "Heads up!"

But it was too late. I wasn't fast enough. I was too wrapped up in my own personal crisis to react before the basketball smashed into my face —*wham!*

I doubled over, my hands flying to where the ball had torpedoed into my eye socket. The pain was sharp—blinding. It took my breath away. Several seconds ticked by before I managed to straighten and inhale, blinking a few times, eyes watering as I searched my surroundings with my good eye like a pirate.

My gaze narrowed, knife-sharp, zeroing in on my assailant. None other than Carson Brooks stood right in my line of vision, a smirk plastered across his perfectly symmetrical pretty-boy face.

I dropped my hand from my throbbing eye and Harper gasped beside me, covering her mouth, mumbling a muffled, "Oh my gosh."

I gave her a cursory glance—she wasn't helping—before I returned my focus back to the court where Carson began to laugh. Not a chuckle, but a bent over at the waist, full on belly roll.

And I snapped.

My hands balled at my side, while I stormed the eight feet separating us to his spot on the court, my eyes blazing, fists at the ready. I was a woman possessed as I closed the gap. All of my problems culminated in the single moment he lobbed the basketball into my face, and I was sure it was him. I had never been more certain of anything in my life. It was always him prodding me, poking me, pricking his needle-sharp jabs under my skin.

My face throbbed where he struck me with the ball, and as I neared, he laughed even harder. It took him but a minute to absorb the fury oozing from my pores, and his laughter faded, morphing into his signature smirk.

I didn't think. I could only react, and before I knew what I was doing, before common sense could prevail, my slender fingers wrapped around his puny neck.

A whistle blew behind me, and far too soon, Mr. Gorby yanked me off of him. "That is enough. Enough!" he yelled. He stood in between us, eyeing me like I was deranged. And maybe I was, because when Carson chuckled again, I made to lunge at him once more.

Mr. Gorby pushed my shoulders back, no longer a teacher but a bouncer in a club, holding back a crazed patron. Behind me, I heard someone —I think it might have been Tasha—mutter, "she's crazy," which was fantastic, really. All I needed to top this crap-show of a day was to have the entire school talking about how I—Mia Randalls—had officially lost my marbles.

I pulled in a shaky breath and yanked on the hem of my blouse, smoothing it with the palm of my hand and lifting my chin, ever the lady, the model student. But as sanity slowly trickled in,

I felt my cheeks heat as I realized the gravity of what I had done.

I had, literally, tried to choke Carson. I mean, sure, he deserved it, but strangling a classmate wasn't exactly something I wanted on my school record, was it?

I mustered as much dignity as I could, avoiding Carson's gaze as Mr. Gorby glared at me. "To the Principal's Office. *Now*."

I heard Carson snicker before the sub turned in his direction and pointed. "Both of you."

Turning, I shot Carson a smug look before the teacher could notice.

"What? Why me?" Carson waved a hand toward me. "She's the one that tried to strangle me."

"Oh, and her eye just swelled up like that on its own?"

My mouth twisted, satisfied. *See, you had it coming*, my face said.

"Fine," Carson muttered.

"Um. Do they maybe need a chaperone?" Harper asked from behind me, sounding a bit scared.

"They'll make it there together just fine. Like civilized people. Am I right?" the substitute asked, though it was more a demand than a question.

I nodded, at least having the decency to look contrite, but when I glimpsed Carson, he smiled like this was all some big joke.

The sub should've let me choke him.

I glared daggers at him as he came up beside me.

"Shorty?" he said, offering his arm to me.

I grimaced, ignoring his arm and the heinous nickname and spun around, heading for the gym doors, putting as much distance between us as possible.

Once I stepped out into the hall, the smack of his tennis shoes over the linoleum soon followed as he hurried to catch up. When he appeared by my side, instead of walking next to me, he pulled ahead.

I narrowed my eyes on his back. He was so tall and his shoulders so broad, I could hardly see past them.

I pumped my arms, moving my feet faster until I was speed-walking past, Carson at my rear. *Ha!*

"What's the hurry, Randalls?" Carson said behind me.

I glanced back, and he seized the opportunity to step in front of me again, but his legs were so long he didn't even look like he was trying. His stride was effortless, natural.

It annoyed me.

I huffed and curled my hands into fists at my side. *Who cares if he walks in front of you? There is no hurry. You do NOT need to get there first. This isn't about winning, Mia.*

I folded my arms over my chest, pushing the bubbling anger aside, trying to focus on something other than Carson's obnoxious swagger.

Oh, who was I kidding?

I took off in a jog, shamelessly smiling at him as I flew past, sending him to my rear where he belonged. Suddenly, our trek to the gallows became a race. When he pulled ahead, I did whatever necessary to beat him. My lungs screamed, but my body vibrated with triumph. I panted as we rounded the corner when Carson called out, "Hey, that's okay. I like the view better from back here anyway."

I stopped dead in my tracks, my feet turning to cement as my head whipped back to see his eyes on my butt. "*Abso-lutely* not," I said.

"What?" He shrugged. "I am a guy, after all, and you actually have a nice—"

"Finish that sentence and you're a dead man," I said, poking him in the ribs as he drew near.

He chuckled and caught my finger in his warm grip.

A zing of electricity shot through my hand

and I yanked it away, shaking it out. Even his touch was weaponized.

"Sorry about your eye," he murmured, his gaze drifting over my face.

"Yeah, you look really sorry."

He raised his hands in surrender, but one corner of his mouth tipped up in a crooked smile. "It was an accident, I swear."

I pursed my lips. The laughter in his voice said otherwise.

Right, an accident, I wanted to say. Like the time he stuck his foot out and tripped me on the way to Ethan's room. I nearly tumbled down the stairs. Or all of the times between classes where he accidentally mowed me down in the hall. Or the way he spilled his drink all over me at lunch just last week.

"It's amazing how a ball accidentally hits me square in the face at lightning speed."

Carson crossed his heart with his finger and held it out.

I rolled my eyes. "Regardless, because of you and your little *accident*, we're headed to Mrs. Parks' office, so thanks for that."

"Actually, I'm pretty sure that was more on account of you trying to strangle me."

My eyes flickered from his face to his neck,

which was slightly mottled. Good. He deserved to have red splotches. My eye felt like it had been attacked by a swarm of bees. I'd be lying if I said I wasn't nervous about assessing the damage, but I wouldn't give Carson the satisfaction of stopping in the bathroom to take a look.

"I wouldn't have wrapped my hands around your neck had you not slammed a basketball in my eye socket."

Carson grinned. "Hey, you know basketball isn't my sport."

I grunted. Everyone knew basketball wasn't his sport. He was the king of Sweet Water's swim team.

"Nice excuse," I said, then began walking again as he hurried to catch up. "You better hope this doesn't get us detention."

Out of the corner of my eye, I noticed his shrug. "It's just detention."

"Just detention? You don't even care that we're in trouble, do you?"

"Won't be the first time. I'm sure it won't be the last."

"Well, isn't that a winning attitude. But this is the first time for me, actually. And it will be the last."

He scowled. "Oh, that's right. I forgot who I was talking to. Can't have anything marring little

Miss Perfect's reputation."

We neared the principal's office, so I paused. "I'm sorry. Some of us have to actually study, get good grades, and have good behavior if we want to succeed. Not all of us can get a free ride just because we know how to swim. Some of us don't have things overlooked simply because we're athletic."

It was an understatement. Carson was a pretty decent cross-country track runner, but he was unrivaled in the water. The boy was born with gills.

He scoffed. "I don't *just* know how to swim."

I smirked as my underhanded dismissal of him hit its mark.

I placed my hands on my hips and watched as he defended his title.

"I've won State two years in a row and set the Sweet Water record in all of my relays. Plus, I plan on breaking all of those again this year."

"You're so modest. I'm surprised you can even swim with that giant ego of yours weighing you down. How does it fit inside your swim cap?"

Carson snorted, and I turned back to the door. Before I could wrench it open, his hand came down over mine. It was big and warm and sent a flurry of nerves jumping in my stomach. I smothered the swell with my annoyance and glanced back at him.

His expression was serious, maybe more so than ever before. "It really was an accident."

I hesitated, staring into eyes the same color as the pool water he practically lived in, and for a moment, I thought he might be genuine.

My gaze raked over his messy dark hair, the hint of facial hair over the sharp edge of his jaw, and his muscular arms, and I swallowed. *Who was I kidding? This was Carson Brooks I was talking about.*

Glancing away from him, I shoved the door open and went inside.

CHAPTER TWO

M rs. Parks stared us down as she wrapped up the phone call I suspected was from the substitute gym teacher. I squirmed in my seat, glancing at Carson from the corner of my eye. He sat with one elbow planted on the arm of the chair, his head resting in his hand like he was bored and had other places to be, like this trip to the principal's office didn't even faze him.

I scowled as I turned my gaze forward again. Four years in this high school and I had never set foot in this office other than to help with something or receive some sort of accolade. Until today.

I bounced my leg as Mrs. Parks placed the

phone back on the receiver, flicking an errant lock of blonde hair from her face. "I have to say, Mia, I'm surprised to see you here," she said.

A wave of shame washed over me, and I bit my lip.

"Carson." Mrs. Parks nodded at him, and I couldn't help but feel slightly smug she hadn't said the same about him.

"Would either of you like to share your side of the story? Mr. Gorby already gave me his account."

I glanced at Carson to see if he was eager to snitch, but he had dropped the hand cradling his head and sat there, eyes trained on his lap. He may be annoying, but he wasn't a tattler, I mused. Well, neither was I.

I pressed my mouth into a tight line, fighting off the words that wanted to escape. *Do you see my face?* I wanted to yell.

"Okay, then." Mrs. Parks lounged back in her chair and tapped her pen on the desk as if thinking of the perfect punishment.

I began to sweat under her scrutiny. Her gaze settled on something behind us, to the corner of the room before it returned back to us and she smiled.

My underarms dampened, and my throat rivaled the Sahara. Why was she looking at us with that excited gleam in her eye? *Oh, no, this wasn't good.*

I said a silent prayer for mercy.

"Technically, you both assaulted each other. That's pretty serious stuff. Normally, for something like this, a suspension would be on the table..."

I felt all the blood drain from my face. *Suspension?*

"But," she continued, "I might have an alternative idea, a little peer remediation, so to speak."

I didn't like the sound of this.

"Remediation?" Carson asked, his forehead crinkling.

I turned to him. "Remediation means the correction of something bad, so—"

"I know what remediation means," he snapped.

A grin curved my lips. "Touchy."

"Kids!" Mrs. Parks banged her hand on the desk. "Can we get along for two seconds?"

We both nodded while stealing guilty glances at each other.

"Every year, as I'm sure you're aware, Sweet Water High sponsors the needy families at Christmastime with the Angel Project. Mrs. Burnham usually coordinates it. She puts up the tree, does all the shopping and organizing, and raises added donations, but she went on maternity leave two weeks ago, leaving us empty handed."

My stomach sunk. *Oh, no...*

"You two," she pointed between us, "will work together to oversee the Angel Project this year. And, remember, Sweet Water families are relying on you."

"But it wasn't my fault." The words burst from my mouth before I could stop them. There was no way I was doing charity work alongside my enemy. Besides, I planned on preparing more essays over break so that if I didn't get accepted for any of the early admissions programs I applied for, I'd have back-ups. That and I still needed to work on a date for the dance.

"Mia, you tried to strangle him." Mrs. Parks' pointed gaze shifted to Carson's neck, then back. "Regardless of whether he threw a ball at you or not, I cannot condone you taking matters into your own hands and assaulting him. Heaven knows there may have been a time or two I've wanted to strangle a student, but..." Her voice trailed off before she cleared her throat and straightened as if remembering who she was talking to. "Physical assault is not condoned at Sweet Water. Ever. You either work on the Angel Project and learn how to get along, or you can have a two-week suspension for the remainder of the semester leading into winter break."

My eyes widened. "But I can't have some-thing like that on my school record. It will affect my college applications. I'm waiting to hear back from—"

"Well, then, it sounds like you've made your decision."

I stared at her for a moment. She looked far too happy about her proposal, which led me to believe she was only thrilled to pawn the charity project off on someone else. One less thing she had to worry about with the holidays looming around the corner.

I glanced over at Carson to see if he was as outraged as I was, and of course, he just sat there, looking like he hadn't a care in the world. When his eye caught mine, he shrugged. "No biggie. We'll do it."

I opened my mouth to speak, to disagree, but I stopped myself. There was no point. I was stuck—cornered. And he knew it, too. There was no way I could have a suspension on my perman-ent record.

I grunted and snapped my mouth shut, cal-culating in my head what this meant in terms of time spent with my nemesis like the convicted calculating their time in jail. Two weeks of plan-ning prior to winter break—gathering supplies, garnering donations, putting the tree up, shopping, and organizing everything. Then there was the delivery of presents and supplies a few days before Christmas.

Ugh. Not only would this mean spending time with him outside of school these next couple weeks, but I'd have to see him over the break as well. I preferred to avoid him as much as possible, which was saying something since his younger brother was my best friend. It took a lot of skills —ones I had perfected over the last nine years—to carefully navigate his house with minimal interaction.

I realized too late Mrs. Parks had been giving instructions during my musing, so I tried to catch up and pay attention.

"Everything you need to know about the current budget is right here," she said, handing a folder to Carson. "Of course, any added donations you can get from local businesses would be great. You want to try to get the most bang for your buck. The Angel Tree will have tags for needy members of the community and for the residents of Sweet Water Nursing Home, but we also adopt five families and provide a full Christmas to them, which is what the food is for. You'll be buying the kids presents, but also everything the families would want or need for Christmas dinner and breakfast—muffins, cookies, juice, coffee. There's a suggested list in there." She pointed toward the folder in Carson's grubby paws, and I glared at him.

The second we exited her office, it was mine. No way was he getting control of this entire thing. I was more organized, the responsible one.

Mrs. Parks cleared her throat, eyeing me as I stared a hole through him, then continued, "You have a week to prepare and start garnering donations, then the tree needs to go up. You'll want to get the food for the families last, just before delivery on the twenty-second. I'll touch base then, over the break. Any questions?"

I forced a smile. "No, ma'am."

Mrs. Parks glanced to Carson, who lazed back in his seat. "Nope. We're good," he answered.

"Good." Mrs. Parks steepled her hands on her desk. "I'm glad you two have agreed to work this thing out between you. I hope you'll learn something from collaborating on this project, maybe make amends."

Blah...Blah...Blah...

I shot to my feet. "May we be dismissed?"

Mrs. Parks nodded and waved toward the door, so I hightailed it out of there. Once I was outside, I waited for Carson. The second he shut the office door behind him, I snatched the folder from his hand. "I'll take that, thank you," I said, opening it and skimming through the contents.

Carson folded his empty hand, then grinned.

His teeth were so white it was abnormal.

Didn't he ever frown?

"Looks like we got off easy," he said.

Easy? *Easy!* I'd hardly call having to work with him from now until Christmas easy. But whatever. If it didn't bother him, then it didn't bother me. I was fine, cool as a cucumber.

"I'll meet you at your house after school," I said.

"Can't. I have an afternoon session today. We have our first meet this weekend."

I scowled. Of course I would have to work around *his* schedule.

"But I could just stop by your place after," he added.

"No!" I yelled, then I inhaled, calming myself. "I mean, I was going to hang with Ethan anyway, so I don't mind coming to your house." The last thing I needed was him showing up to my place and my parents having an epic throw-down.

I tipped my chin up. "How about seven? Does that suit your busy schedule?"

Carson pursed his lips like he was thinking it over, and I tried not to notice how full they were. The gesture did funny things to my insides.

"Sure. That works," he drawled, then winked and brushed past me, bumping my shoulder in the process, and just when I was about to tell him, *excuse you*, he turned my way and saluted. "Seven it is," he said.

I waited a moment, allowing the irritation to dissipate from my bloodstream like a drug, wondering how one person could be so infuriating. When I turned to stomp off in the other direction, I crashed into something solid. *Oomph.*

I stumbled back, then blinked up to see Ethan and nearly collapsed in relief. If there was one person I wanted to run into right now, it was my best friend.

His amber eyes went wide as the moon as he took in my face. "What the heck happened to you?"

I frowned. "Your brother happened. I can't believe the two of you came from the same womb. Are you sure you're biologically related? Maybe your mother had an illicit affair she never told you about," I said as I headed toward my locker. If I wanted to make it to Spanish on time, I'd better hurry.

"Uh, not likely," Ethan called after me, and I knew it was true. Mr. and Mrs. Brooks were nothing short of the perfect couple. They were attached at the hip, real-life examples that true love existed, unlike my own parents.

"Why did you have to be born a year younger? It would be so much easier if you were the older one, then it would be you that I shared classes with, not the animal you call a brother." I stopped at my locker and hurriedly turned the combination lock, then popped it open.

Ethan leaned against the locker next to mine, his sandy-colored hair flopping in his eyes. If he weren't like a brother to me, he'd be kinda cute. "Uh, do I really need to explain how conception works?" he said.

I couldn't help but grin.

"So, let me get this straight, Carson did that to you? For real?"

I grabbed my Spanish textbook and slammed my locker door, then headed down the hall again. "Yep."

"Maybe you should go see the nurse."

I stopped, and we nearly collided again. Ethan only had a handful of inches on me, unlike Carson, who was over a foot taller. My hand shot out before we could clash skulls. A headbutt to the face was all I needed.

A freshman behind us muttered something unfriendly as she went around us. Ignoring her, I eyed Ethan warily. "Why would I go to the nurse?" I mean, it hurt, but how bad could it be?

Ethan winced as he spun me around, toward

the glass pane of a classroom door. It took a moment for me to realize what he was doing until my eyes focused on my reflection. With a yelp, I jumped at my shadowy image, then crept closer.

"You have got to be kidding me," I hissed.

My heart banged in my chest as I took in the damage. My right eye had swollen half shut, and even from the blurry image of myself in the glass, I could tell it was bruised. *How on earth am I going to fix this?*

"Great. Just great," I said, hearing the emotion in my voice.

I was going to lose it for the second time that morning. I was two seconds away from having an emotional breakdown. "Now I'll never find a date to the Snowflake Ball." Tears of frustration stung the back of my eyes, but I refused to let my emotions get the best of me.

I inhaled a shaky breath and rolled my shoulders back.

I have this under control. I've totally got this. It was nothing a little ice and concealer—okay, a LOT of concealer—couldn't fix. It's not the end of the world.

"Let's take a moment," Ethan said, sensing my rising hysteria.

He grabbed me by the shoulders and steered me back toward the lockers.

"But Spanish..." I mumbled half-heartedly.

Ethan raised a brow. "I'm pretty sure once your teacher sees your face, you'll be excused for being a couple minutes late."

I nodded. That thought shouldn't comfort me, but it did.

"Why don't you start by filling me in on exactly what happened. Then, when you're done, I'll punch my brother square in the face. Deal?"

A small spurt of laughter escaped my lips before it faded, and I began to fill Ethan in on what happened at gym class and my ensuing punishment from Mrs. Parks.

"You really tried to strangle Carson?"

I nodded. "Yeah. It was pretty bad now that I think about it."

Ethan laughed like it was the funniest thing he'd ever heard. "That's classic. Totally savage. Man, I wish I could've been there to see his face."

"Yeah, well. Thanks to my little retaliation, I'm stuck working with him for the next three weeks. Talk about punishment. So, not only do I have to deal with being dateless, silence on my college applications, my parent's escalating fights, *and* having to spend my spare time with the enemy, but I get to do it all looking like a cyclops."

"Oh, come on. It's not that bad." Ethan pressed his lips in a tight line as his gaze lingered over my right eye. "Okay, maybe it is that bad, but

27

it'll get better in a couple days."

I glared at him. "Thanks a lot. You're the best friend a girl could ask for."

"Hey, in all seriousness, Carson isn't terrible. Working with him isn't the worst punishment."

I shot him a skeptical look.

"Really. Maybe this little assignment will finally help you two get along. It would be nice not to have to hide you when we're hanging out at my house all the time."

"Doubtful," I muttered. "I'm supposed to meet him tonight at seven."

"Why don't you come over early and have dinner with my family, get out of your house, away from your parents?"

Away from the war zone. He didn't have to say it for me to catch his meaning.

"You don't think your mom and dad would mind?" I asked, hoping he'd say no, because a decent dinner without the loaded silence settling between my parents sounded like heaven.

"Are you kidding? My parents love you. They'd adopt you if they could."

I smiled and slung my bookbag back over my shoulder when Ethan wrapped his arm around my shoulders. Already things were looking up.

"And, hey," he said, nodding to me, "don't worry about the dance. You'll get a date, I promise. Then we'll double and have a blast."

"Easy for you to say. You have a hot date." I pouted.

I knew Ethan would cancel his plans if I asked him to. He was that loyal. But I would never do that to him. There was no point in ruining his life just because mine sucked at the moment. It was bad enough he had to live with Carson and see him every day. I wouldn't spoil his love life, too. He'd been stoked when Beth said yes to going with him.

The bell for the final period rang, and so I started to back away. "I'll see you tonight," I said and walked off.

I'd work this all out. Somehow.

CHAPTER THREE

After giving Ethan a ride home, I headed down Tidewater Street toward my own house. The scent of the ocean permeated the soft breeze off the water. Though it was cool, the air was damp and the sound of the gulls in the distance weirdly comforting. My family didn't live right off the beach, but we were only a short ten-minute drive to the waterfront. Our location had its perks—far enough off the main drag we didn't deal with the summer traffic on the way to the beach, close enough we could go swimming any time we wanted, yet only a short drive to downtown Sweet Water as well.

This time of year, everything was dead. Come November, a good majority of restaurants and little shops in Sweet Water were boarded up, lights off, closed down for the winter. Even the little bowling alley and the mini golf closed its doors for a few months. The weather was colder and the local business wasn't enough to keep them alive. It was a relative ghost town compared to midsummer. If it weren't for the coastal air and the beautiful weather, I would've probably gone stir crazy long ago. Sometimes quiet was good, and other times, it let your thoughts circulate way too easily.

I arrived home quickly since there was no traffic, a side effect of December in Sweet Water and not the time of day. Tourists wouldn't start coming to town until May. Even then, the majority of vacationers stayed June through August, with a trickling of tourists throughout September and October. In July, the route from Sweet Water High to home could take more than twenty minutes due to traffic. Today, it took less than ten, which meant I found myself to and from Ethan's, back at home, far too soon.

I got out of my car, unlocked the front door, and headed straight for my room. It wouldn't be long until my mother arrived home, and I wasn't exactly looking forward to our impending conversation about my little trip to the Principal's Office. Mrs. Parks was nothing if not thorough, and there was no doubt in my mind she had informed my parents of my antics.

I dropped my bookbag by my bedroom door, then opened it up, removing the file folder with the information Mrs. Parks gave us on the Angel Project. Stopping at my dresser on the way to my desk, I assessed my appearance with a grimace. Some swelling had gone down, but the area surrounding my eye was undoubtedly bruised and puffy. The contrast to my milky skin was startling. Unfortunately for me, I was one of those people who barely got a tan. I went from white to burnt like a crisp in the blink of an eye. And I hated when I got sunburned because it brought out the red in my hair, giving it this weird pink lemonade appearance, while I much preferred to emphasize the blonde.

The damage could be worse, I supposed, but I was half tempted to grab my makeup bag and do a little concealing before I realized my appearance would only help plead my case of temporary insanity to my parents.

I didn't know when Carson and I became rivals. Okay, that was a lie. It's funny how the mind worked. I couldn't remember what I had for lunch three days ago, but I had a very distinct memory of the day I first met the Brooks boys—polar opposites in personality, as well as their impending roles in my life—one destined to be my best friend and the other my nemesis.

Although they lived around the corner from me, we met on the beach. I was only nine years old at the time. My mother started talking to their family first. They were new in town, moved here from Chicago in search of surf and sand and the temperate weather North Carolina had to offer. Theoretically, one would think I would've gravitated toward Carson since he was my age, doomed to be in the same class for the rest of our Sweet Water years. Our mothers even remarked on it. But the way things are supposed to work out and the way they actually do are often two very different things.

I remembered noticing Carson in the water. Even then, he was a veritable fish. He flopped around, dove, and splashed in the waves like a dolphin, while Ethan and I played in the sand. Eventually, the ninety-degree heat and the blazing sun took their toll, and I needed to cool off, so I ventured into the water cautiously, dipping down in a soft swell, allowing the saltwater to cool me. But before I could run back out of the surf, a hand caught my leg. I looked back into Carson's smiling face. He was floating on his red boogie board with a crooked smile. His dark hair was a little lighter and a little longer back then. It always hung in his eyes, and I found myself continually wanting to brush it away.

The sun glistened off his boyish frame, yet to be broadened and muscled from puberty and years of swimming. He had a small smattering of freckles just over his nose. Ones I knew only cropped up in the summer. But it was his eyes that transfixed me, even then—all that vast blue.

I hadn't seen the wave coming. It crashed down over me just as Carson pushed off, propelled by the momentum on his board, riding the wave, while I practically drowned in it. The undertow sucked me down until I rolled over the sand, the waves tumbling my body like a piece of shale. When I finally surfaced, gasping for air, I pushed the hair out of my face, coughing and choking up salty water. My belly burned from its brutal encounter with sand and shells. My throat was raw, my skin red, and when I looked up at Carson, lying peacefully on the sand, still on his board, blissful after his ride on the waves, I frowned. He glanced back at me and laughed. LAUGHED!

Now, I was no expert at nine, but I was pretty sure laughing when someone nearly lost their life *because of you* was not the proper way to make friends. Call me crazy.

"You were supposed to swim," he said.

Swim—as if it were that simple.

Yeah, I wanted to say, *sure*. Your eyes tranquilized me, but my little nine-year-old brain was supposed to be cognizant enough to see the wave coming (from the eyes in the back of my head I didn't know I had). Right.

I stared daggers at him. It was Ethan who ran to my side and saved me. He grabbed my hand and asked if I was okay, then offered me some of his sports drink and Swedish Fish. And I never forgot it.

It was the first and last time Carson Brooks would ensnare me.

With the memory of that day fresh in my mind, I headed to my desk, marveling at how our rivalry only grew from there. Grabbing my laptop, I carried it over to my bed, where I propped myself up against my upholstered headboard with a bunch of pillows and stretched my legs out in front of me.

I booted my computer and clicked on the link in my favorites—the only link worth saving—and the website for Duke University loaded. I let my gaze scan the screen, scrolling through the pictures with a yearning so deep it hurt. By the time I was finished, my head ached, and my mood had darkened perceptibly.

Where was my acceptance letter?

I had called last week, and sure enough, the woman in admissions had ensured me they had begun sending them out.

I dropped my head in my hands, pressing my palms into my eyes. I'd get in, I told myself. I had to.

Shake it off.

Opening the folder Mrs. Parks gave us, I removed the contents, surprised to find more than the sheets she had gone over in her office. There was a lot of valuable information inside—lists of supplies they'd need, pictures from last year's program to give them an idea on how much food the families received, what the tree looked like upon completion, and suggested lists of items to buy.

A plan began to form in my head as I laid everything out around me, then opened a spreadsheet on my laptop. I could divvy up the tasks. That way, Carson could take on a few things, and I'd do the rest. There was no need for us to work on it together when we could easily divide and conquer. Why take three weeks to complete the tasks when I could probably finish most of it myself in a few days if I put my mind to it?

I compiled a master list of supplies in my spreadsheet, then divided them up and labeled one file "Mia" and the other "Carson." Once he gave me his share of goods, I'd gather them all together and make the boxes. In the meantime, I could probably manage the Angel Tree myself. No need for him to help with all of it. He'd be busy with the swim team, anyway. Then we could each deliver our own boxes with little interaction. Easy.

I sighed contentedly and closed my eyes, sinking into the plush headboard. It had been a stressful day. Maybe if I just rested for a minute before my parents got home, before I needed to meet with Carson...

I drifted to sleep, awakening sometime later to the sound of the front door slamming. I became alert immediately, tensing as I stared out into the hallway, waiting.

And there it was, only a moment later my mother's voice cut through the air like the starting bell in a boxing ring. "This is your fault," she snarled.

I didn't need to be down there to know who she was speaking to.

"Oh, of course, it's my fault. Everything's my fault!" Dad yelled.

Round one, let the games begin.

My stomach twisted with dread. The moment I heard the sound of my name—something about me "acting out"—I knew this particular argument was about me.

Fantastic.

As if their fighting weren't awful enough, being the root of it was even worse.

I headed downstairs, despite everything inside me screaming to ignore them, to put my headphones on and drown them out with something loud and upbeat. But it was time for me to head over to the Brooks' house, which meant I needed to face the music if I wanted to see Ethan and have a quiet dinner before meeting Carson.

My feet hit the landing, and I stood to the side of where they faced-off like two bulldogs. It took them a whole two minutes and me clearing my throat for them to even realize I was there. During moments like these, it was hard to reconcile them to the loving couple I remember from when I was younger. The one who took me on family vacations, swam with me at the beach, and planned family barbecues.

My mother turned to me and visibly deflated. I noticed the flicker of remorse in her eyes and the way my father snapped his mouth shut and stared at the ground, ashamed. They hated when I caught them in the middle of a fight, which both annoyed and amused me because I wanted to ask them if they thought I was deaf—I would have to be to miss their sparring.

"Your eye," my mother said. Her gaze flickered over my face.

My father shot her a disgusted look, then said, "Mrs. Parks told us you tried to strangle Carson Brooks. Is that true?"

Yikes. *When they put it that way...*

I reached for the hem of my shirt and twisted it between my fingers. "Not entirely."

"Not entirely?" My mother frowned. "Did he do this to you? Did he give you a black eye?"

"Well, it's not really a black eye, just a little bruising." What was I saying? I wanted them to feel sorry for me, and I wanted the blame on Carson.

Balance. I needed to find balance, which usually rested somewhere between the truth and a lie. I needed middle ground.

"He hit me with a basketball."

"On purpose?" Mom asked, crossing her arms over her chest.

"Well," I drawled, "it was meant to get my attention, but his aim was off, and he hit me square in the face."

"And your part in all this was?" My father asked.

"Um... The impact kind of blinded me for a moment. I was so surprised, and it hurt pretty bad, so I stumbled my way toward him." *More like loped my way in an angry rage.* "And I intended to shove him, but somehow my hands went around his neck instead." I winced.

Wow. I was really winning at this lying thing.

"You're trying to say you *accidentally* tried to choke him?" My mother asked, brows raised.

I hesitated. This sounded like a trick question. One that could get me into more trouble.

"It was more like a playful shove in the trachea." I held out a finger. "Also an accident."

My parents glanced at each other, and I swore for a moment, I saw a spark of amusement, like they both wanted to burst out laughing. And if this were five years ago, maybe they would've. But not anymore. They found humor in nothing, least not with each other, which extended to me as well. Because wasn't I a part of both of them, an amalgamation of their love? I was merely a reminder of what once was. Nowadays, if one was happy, the other was automatically mad. If one was hot, the other was cold. When one was hungry, the other lost their appetite. It was exhausting. Most days I wondered how they were still standing.

"Mrs. Parks said she handled it and that the two of you are doing a peer remediation project?" Dad asked, and really, the project was perfect because judging by his rigid stance, he wanted to punish me. And Dad's "go-to" had always been grounding me, something he couldn't entirely do if I needed to meet up with Carson to work on the project, and if I just so happened to run into Ethan on the way, well...

"Yeah." I stepped forward, smiling. "Actually, that's where I'm headed now. We're working on the Sweet Water Angel Program and the Angel Tree for Christmas." I glanced to my wrist a moment too late, realizing I hadn't worn my watch today. I shook my arm uselessly. "Uh, I was supposed to leave five minutes ago."

Dad sighed and glanced to Mom one last time. "Fine. But I'm going to call Mrs. Parks in a week and make sure you're doing everything required of you."

Just when I thought I'd gotten off easy, he said, "And no going out for the next two weeks, other than to work on the project. It's school, the project, and your room. Got it?"

I nodded mutely.

"That seems a bit harsh," Mom said. "Look at her face, and I'm sure if she's not doing what's expected, Mrs. Parks will give us a call."

"Oh, I'm sorry, Penny. I forgot. We should just let our daughter get away with assaulting other kids. Great parenting."

"She's best friends with his brother, I highly doubt—"

"Yeah, speaking of which, I was never fond of how you thrust those two together. She's an eighteen-year-old girl. Her best friend should be another girl."

Mom snorted. "What is this, 1940? She can't be best friends with a boy? According to you, the opposite sex can be just friends and coworkers. Or, are you just blowing smoke?"

"Of course, you're going to turn this

around..."

With a resigned sigh, I hurried from the room, letting the sound of their arguing float away, fading into the distance.

It was amazing how good I'd gotten at blocking them out.

Normally, I drove to Ethan's house, but today, I decided to walk. The temperature was mild, nearly fifty-six degrees, so I knew my hoodie and jeans would suffice. It was only fifteen minutes by foot, and I desperately needed to clear my head, to shake off the aftereffects of my parent's fighting.

I breathed in the fresh air, enjoying the simple sensation of filling my lungs until bursting, then releasing the pressure. It was the same feeling I got at home, like I was filling up-up-and-up until I thought I might explode.

I pulled the drawstrings of my hoodie tighter, taking in the Christmas lights, pine wreaths, and garland decorating the surrounding homes when it dawned on me—my parents hadn't put up any decorations this year. We hadn't even gotten our Christmas tree up yet, and while Christmas was still three weeks away, we usually put it up after Thanksgiving. What did that even mean, the absence of those things?

I glanced to my right at the sound of laughter and watched as a family—mother, father, and two daughters—piled out of a car and headed into a light-trimmed house. A stab of envy sunk inside my bones. I wanted desperately to be a part of a real family again. Happy. Carefree. Going places together and then returning home with nothing but joy and contentedness, but instead, I found myself constantly walking on eggshells, always trying to be perfect, to find something to make my parents happy again—to bring us back together. And look where that got me. All my problems were building and rising to the surface, threating to spill out of me in one cataclysmic eruption, and today they finally had. When that ball hit me and I saw Carson laugh, I snapped.

I embarrassed myself in front of the class.

I almost got suspended.

I was unraveling. And I knew it.

I couldn't keep up the pretense much longer, but I had to try. For them. For us. For myself, at least until I left for school in the fall. *If* I left for school in the fall. I still hadn't gotten any early acceptance letters yet. I checked the mail before I left the house—twice just to be sure.

With the way things had been going lately, it would be my luck to get rejected from all the colleges I applied to and be forced to stay right there in Sweet Water. The only bright side to that terrifying scenario would be an extra year with Ethan. He was my best friend, and so the only downside to going away to school was leaving him behind. Because he was a Sweet Water lifer. He'd never leave.

The Brooks' house came into view with their large, sunny yellow exterior, their huge white wraparound porch, and the wind chimes that seemed to endlessly tinkle a cheerful, melodic tune. Above the garage was a giant, brightly painted sign with a grand sailboat created by a local artist. It read, "Welcome to Port," and that's exactly how I felt as I approached—home, at bay.

I started to veer into their driveway when a sleek black car I recognized as Olivia's slowed next to me and came to a stop. When Olivia poked her head out of the window, she smiled. "Hey, Mia."

"Uh, hi," I said.

I was reasonably popular but tended to float between groups, never associating myself with any one clique. Instead, I socialized with a smattering of kids from all circles at Sweet Water High, which meant I wasn't unfriendly with Olivia, but she wasn't exactly one of my favorite people either. She and Tasha tended to look down on a lot of people, and their favorite pastime seemed to be hopping from boy to boy. No one was off limits. The word man-eater came to mind. When Greg dumped me my sophomore year, it was amazing how Olivia had conveniently been there for him in his time of need. A day later, they were an item. Olivia and Tasha were always nice to my face, but I always wondered what they said about me behind closed doors. I suspected it was as cruel as what they said about everyone else.

"So, that was pretty crazy today in gym." Her eyes sparkled with laughter, and I was no body language expert, but something told me she had an ulterior motive for this bit of small talk.

"Yeah." I shrugged and crossed my arms over my chest.

"I mean, if I were you, I'd be totally mortified. The way you went after Carson like that." She widened her eyes. "And your face. I mean, yikes."

My hand automatically shot up to my eye. I dropped it, not wanting to give her the satisfaction of getting under my skin. With girls like Olivia, it was all about not letting them see you sweat.

I pursed my lips. Did she actually want me to respond? What did she expect me to say? "Yeah, it wasn't my finest moment. But Carson is always picking on me, and he kind of had it coming."

"I heard you have to do that lame Christmas tree thing together now." She grimaced, then added, "But at least you get to be punished together. I mean, Carson's pretty hot. I heard he hasn't asked anyone to the Snowflake Ball yet."

Is there a point to this, I wanted to ask, but I kept my mouth shut and glanced back to the Brooks' house then to Olivia again, hoping she got the hint. "Right. Um, did you need anything? I'm kind of running late. I'm supposed to meet Ethan..."

"Of course. Yeah, actually, that's why I stopped when I saw you. I know you're, like, best friends with his brother or whatever...I mean, I don't know why. He's an underclassman." She pulled a face like she couldn't imagine anything worse.

"He's a junior."

"Whatever. I just thought since you're tight with the other Brooks kid that you could, you know, mention me to Carson. Maybe mention the dance, too. I thought he might want to—"

"The other Brooks kid's name is Ethan, and don't you already have a date?"

Olivia's smile froze on her perfect face. "Well, I didn't give any of them a *hard* yes."

She couldn't be serious. But wait, this was Olivia, so of course, she was.

"Uh-huh. I'll be sure to let him know you're interested," I said, hoping I didn't sound as bitter as I felt. Only Carson could act like a jerk and snag a date. Then again, he seemed to only reserve his toxic charm for me.

"Great." Olivia flashed me one of her super-model smiles, then rolled her window back up and drove off.

I gave her an epic eye roll once she was gone, but it wasn't enough to smother the hot and sticky feeling settling inside my chest. Why did I care that Olivia wanted to go to the dance with Carson? They'd look good together. And he probably liked the vapid, materialistic type.

Turning back, I headed up the driveway and onto the porch. I paused at the front door, listening to the muffled sounds from inside. Music played softly in the background, and Ethan's voice vibrated through the door, followed by his parents' laughter, and the clinking of dishes as they set the table. The scent of tomato sauce wafted toward me from an open window in the kitchen. Mrs. Brooks was famous for having a window open, no matter the weather. She said fresh air was good for the soul. I just thought the Brooks family was good for the soul. Well, most of them, anyway.

"You're early."

The sound of Carson's voice startled the smile from my face. I brought a hand up to my racing heart and swiveled around to face him.

He approached the stairs, taking them slowly in that unhurried air he always had about him, and I couldn't help but wonder what it would feel like to be so relaxed all the time, so nonchalant about life. Once he neared the top step, he paused, so we were almost at eye level, both of us facing off, lost in our own thoughts.

His hair was still damp from swim practice. A pair of goggles dangled from his grasp, along with a Wild Cats duffle bag that I imagined contained a change of clothes. The soft cotton of his long sleeve t-shirt clung to the hard plains of his chest, while the swell of his biceps strained against his shirtsleeves, toned from hours in the pool and the gym lifting weights.

Realizing I was staring, I wrenched my eyes I away. It was probably the longest either of us had ever gone without speaking in each other's presence. Usually, we were racing to the punchline, trying to see who could offer the most snark. When I finally slid my eyes to his, he was already watching me, his mouth curling in amusement.

I cleared my throat and mumbled, "Your brother invited me for dinner."

"Ah. And here I thought you were just eager to see me." His grin broadened, and he took another step. One more and he'd be close enough to touch.

I shot him a warning glare. From this height, I was almost as tall as him. It was weird being able to see him from this level, and I relished the power the extra six inches gave me.

A soft breeze drifted between us, ruffling the front of his dark hair. I opened my mouth to say something smart, one of my typical biting remarks reserved only for him when the scent of his body wash drifted toward me, rendering me mute.

"Take a picture, it'll last longer." Carson winked.

I scoffed. "Creative. How long did it take you to think up that one?"

"About as long as you were staring at me, so a while."

I narrowed my eyes. "Please. I was just trying to figure out who you looked more like, Sloth from the Goonies or The Elephant Man."

Carson grinned. "Funny." Then he reached out and tugged on a loose wisp of my hair. "What color is this, anyway? I think I've had vomit the same shade."

I crossed my arms, hugging my fists to my chest. "Nope. I should know. I puke looking at you almost every day."

"Could you be any shorter?" He raised a brow, staring me down, and I fought the urge to stand on my tiptoes. I would not give him the satisfaction. The hair was a low blow, but I was used to him mocking my height.

"I'm almost as tall as you."

He arched a brow, sliding his gaze down my

body. "You're standing on the stair above me."

I harrumphed, ignoring my mistake, and hating the way it felt like he was just checking me out. "How'd you do? Drown anyone in the water today?" I asked, motioning toward his bag and goggles.

He followed my eyes and glanced back up. "You weren't there, remember? But if you're so interested, I smoked everyone." He grinned. "I've got State in the bag again this year."

I nodded wordlessly. Of course he did. Was there anything he was bad at?

Carson took the final step until he stood right in front of me, forcing me to tip my head back to meet his eyes, miles above mine. It was such a disadvantage, being small.

He reached his free hand out toward the bruise below my eye and I flinched. For a moment, I thought he was going to deliver the final death blow. Our rivalry would end right there on his front porch. But instead, he gently brushed a fingertip over the sensitive skin. I swallowed, frozen, and afraid this was some sort of mind game. Just in case, I couldn't let my guard down an inch.

"Look, Mia, I—"

"Hey, Mia, when'd you get—" Ethan flung the front door open, cutting Carson off.

I leaped away from him so fast, a wave of vertigo hit me, and I stumbled. My head spun. I flailed for balance, trying uselessly to steady myself when a set of strong arms wrapped around me.

CHAPTER FOUR

*T*hese were not *the arms of my best friend.*

Nope. I've felt those arms—slightly wiry, familiar, comforting. Instead, these were hard and muscled, so long I wouldn't be surprised if they could wrap around my tiny body twice. *That was probably his plan, squeeze me like a boa constrictor until I give.*

I quickly righted myself and took a step back as if Carson had caught fire, knowing Ethan was watching, his gaze heavy on the side of my face.

I curled my upper lip. "Ugh. Any excuse to touch me. Who knows where those arms have been." Likely wrapped around someone like

Olivia.

Carson snorted and stepped forward, flicking a lock of my hair, and hovering close to my face like one of those annoying gnats that circle the fruit bowl in the summer. "How cute. You're still in the boys-have-cooties phase."

"Not all boys. Just you."

When Carson laughed in return, and I stuck my tongue out at him, basically proving his point. It was terribly juvenile, and I resented him for reducing me to the level of a grade-schooler.

I flashed Ethan a genuine smile, thankful for his presence. "Hey," I said, running a hand through my hair, composing myself.

Ethan's silence spoke volumes as he arched his brow and glanced between us. "Everything okay out here?"

"Yeah. Of course. We were just talking about our project. Everything is perfectly fine. Why wouldn't it be?" I asked, wondering why I couldn't just shut up.

"That's funny. I don't remember us discussing the project just now," Carson chimed in.

See? Gnat.

"Did I ask you?" I snapped.

"Whatever," Ethan interrupted our glaring match. "Things are never just fine with you two, but I'm used to it by now. You coming in or what?"

With more force than necessary, I brushed past Ethan and stepped inside, inhaling the scent of sauce and cheese. "Please tell me your mom made her lasagna."

"You're in luck." Ethan placed his hands on my shoulders and guided me toward the dining room.

"I'm just going to drop my stuff in my room," Carson called from behind us, and though I shouldn't, I felt a little surge of joy that no one seemed to care.

I took my undesignated-designated seat at the table, the one beside Ethan, accepting Mrs. Brooks' offer of lemonade, and making small talk as she set a giant bowl of tossed salad on the table. After she took her seat next to Mr. Brooks, Carson appeared a moment later and sat directly across from me, his gaze cool on my face.

We said grace, as was customary there, a nice reprieve to the tense silence at my own dinner table, then filled our plates.

I took a bite of lasagna and scarcely avoided moaning in pleasure when Mrs. Brooks glanced over to me, a timid expression on her face. "Mia, honey, I hate to ask this, but I can't avoid it any longer. What on earth happened to your eye?"

The bite of food turned to mush in my

mouth. My probing gaze shot to Carson, who hung his head, staring at his food with the intensity of a neurosurgeon, while Ethan choked on a forkful of salad. "Oh, you didn't hear?" I asked.

"No." Mrs. Brooks looked to both of her sons, somehow sensing they had something to do with it.

Ask Carson, I wanted to say. Instead, I narrowed my eyes on him for a moment, and either I imagined it, or his cheeks were turning red.

Interesting. Carson Brooks blushing? That was a first.

"It happened in gym class," I said, enjoying Carson's tortured anticipation of me outing him.

I had no idea how the Brooks had not received the same call from Mrs. Parks, but having something to hang over Carson's head might be kind of fun. For once, I had the upper hand.

Mrs. Brooks put her fork down, her forehead wrinkled in concern. "Did you fall?"

Ethan spluttered beside me, then covered his laughter with his fist.

"Actually, a boy threw a ball at my face. Right here"—I pointed at my eye—"in the orbital and zygomatic bone."

"The *what*?" Ethan asked, looking amused.

Across the table, Carson sneered and

mouthed, *Dork.*

Mr. Brooks frowned. "On purpose?"

"Yeah."

Her eyes darkened. "Oh, dear," Mrs. Brooks said. "What is wrong with kids these days? If he was my son, I could promise you, he'd regret even thinking of hitting a lady in the face with a ball. I mean, who does that for no reason? Animals. Kids are animals. I told you, George," she turned to Mr. Brooks, "we should've homeschooled."

Carson's lips quirked at that, laughter sparkling in his eyes as he met my gaze.

"Yeah, who does that?" I asked, my lips twitching.

"How do you know it was on purpose? That's a pretty big presumption," Carson said.

I scoffed. "Puh-lease. Like his aim is that bad. It was going ninety-miles-per-hour right at my face. The opposite direction of the hoop, I might add."

"Ninety miles an hour, huh? Wow." Carson widened his eyes comically. "Who is this kid? We need to call some scouts. Hurry, get the manager for the Charlotte Hornets on the phone. This kid could play for the NBA right now."

I trained my eyes on his face, loading my icy blue laser beams. He thought he was so clever and cute.

"Not funny," Mr. Brooks said, but he grinned, and his tone said otherwise.

Carson covered his smile with his napkin, and just as I turned to Mrs. Brooks, ready to deliver the final blow, to reveal it was actually *him*, he said, "Mia, I'm curious. What did you do after the ball hit you?"

I froze, the words on the tip of my tongue. "I don't see how that's relevant," I said, then took a small bite of lasagna.

"Some people—Mrs. Parks—for one, might disagree. I think we need the full story here. I sense something is missing. Some other piece of the story." He folded his hands under his face, looking completely innocent—he was a counselor gently coaxing their patient.

"I don't think—"

"Humor us," he said.

I pursed my lips, hoping the heat radiating off of me might make him spontaneously combust.

"Oh, honey. Did you cry?" Mrs. Brooks reached over and squeezed my hand. "It's okay if you did. I remember the time I got spiked in the face with a volleyball in junior high. Brought instant tears to my eyes. No one will remember tomorrow."

Carson mashed his lips together, his entire

body vibrating with the effort of holding in his laughter, but he failed. He burst out laughing, and even Ethan, next to me, couldn't help himself. Traitor.

Tiny crystalline tears collected in Carson's eyes as he struggled to speak. I wouldn't be surprised if they dropped from his eyes ice-cold like his heart. "Well, did you, Mia? Did you cry? Or did you—"

I slouched down in my chair and kicked him under the table, cutting him off.

"Ow," he hissed, and I turned up my nose, glancing to Mrs. Brooks.

Poor Mrs. Brooks. She avoided my gaze. Clearly, she thought I was embarrassed because I cried, not because I tried to strangle her son with my bare hands. If I only I would've had more time.

I grunted something unintelligible, then loaded lasagna into my mouth, one angry bite at a time. The only thing that made me feel the slightest bit better was when Mrs. Brooks swatted the boys with the salad tongs on the back of the head for still laughing, warning them they'd better eat their supper.

After dinner, Carson cleared the table while Mrs. Brooks wrapped up the leftovers, and I helped Ethan load the dishwasher.

He handed me a rinsed dish, which I placed

in the washer. "Looking forward to working with Carson?"

I groaned. "That's like asking me if I'm looking forward to having a tooth pulled. Only there's no Novocain where Carson's concerned."

"Come on. It didn't look like you two were all that uncomfortable when I found you outside. You were standing pretty close. It actually looked kind of—"

"Like I was trying to keep the contents of my stomach down? Ready for a round two replay of this afternoon in gym class?" I smiled at him sweetly.

He shook his head and laughed. "You two never change. What'll I do next year without you guys? It'll be so boring."

"Transfer high schools for your senior year to Durham?"

"Still hoping to get into Duke?"

"Yep."

Ethan held out a handful of silverware, which I took from him. He opened his mouth to say something before he stopped, and I tilted my head. Arching a brow, I asked, "What?"

"Nothing. Never mind. I'm sure you'll get in though."

"I hope so." I began separating the silverware. "Do you want to sit in on our little brain-storm sesh? It'll be fun," I promised. "You can be the buffer, so we don't kill each other."

"As exciting as that sounds, I was headed over to the girls' basketball game tonight. I heard Beth was going to be there, so I thought I'd scope it out."

I deflated a little, then pumped myself up. I was his best friend, so I needed to act like it. "Ooh, so somebody's trying to make this about more than just a dance."

"Maybe," Ethan said, and his cheeks pinkened.

I felt an instant pang of sympathy. While Carson was the life of the party and a pot-stirrer, Ethan was painfully shy and kind of nerdy. The only thing cool about him by high school stand-ards was the fact that he played football. He hadn't done much more than go on a few group dates in the past, so pursuing a girl was huge for him.

"Well, she'd be crazy not to go after you," I said, reaching out and squeezing his arm.

"Thanks."

From the entrance to the kitchen, someone cleared their throat. I glanced over to see Carson's gaze, homing in on us as Ethan blushed.

"You ready or what?" Carson said, his tone tight.

I frowned at him. Did he have to be so rude? I threw the kitchen towel down on the counter and sighed.

"Ugh. Whatever." I stepped forward and gave Ethan a hug, whispering, "Go get the girl," in his ear before giving him a squeeze and stepping away.

"Take me to your dungeon," I said, but instead of finding the joke funny, Carson scowled the whole way upstairs toward his room.

I wasn't sure what I expected Carson's bedroom to be like. Maybe painted black, quiet like a tomb, with little pint-sized voodoo dolls sporting strawberry-blonde hair and pins sticking out of them. I expected something cold and slightly sinister, booby-traps around every corner, a book of spells he liked to inflict on his nemesis (me). He was always so careful when I hung out with Ethan, room sealed up tight as a drum. I tried to break into it once when Ethan was in the bathroom. It was as impenetrable as Fort Knox.

Instead, my jaw dropped at what I found.

Ethan's room I knew as well as my own. Where his room was slightly messy, practical, dark, and masculine, Carson's was surprisingly bright and tidy. And it was one giant ode to swimming.

In short, it was incredible.

Scanning the room in awe, I stepped further inside, taking in the shelves above his desk showcasing trophies and medals he'd been awarded over the years, mostly swimming, with a smattering of cross-country. When I inhaled, the same masculine scent of body wash from outside filled my lungs.

I turned and smiled at the giant poster above his bed that read, "Eat. Sleep. Swim. Repeat." Next to it, another framed photo read, "Chlorine, the breakfast of champions." But as I approached his bed—a bed made for a giant— the cheeky artwork wasn't what caught my eye. What made me pause was the large canvas next to it, above his nightstand. It was a massive photograph of a swimmer, his arms raised, poised above the water. The detail was so incredible, you felt like you were there watching. The muscles in his shoulders tensed, flexed in the still-life photo, ready to power through the surface, his face only partially visible as he took a breath. And even with the water, goggles, and the swim cap partially obscuring his features, I recognized the man in the image in an instant.

In that single photograph, you could see the raw power in Carson's arms, his love for the sport. You could sense his speed, his drive. I could feel the icy water sloshing in the pool and taste the chlorine.

"My mom took it and had it blown up," he murmured from behind.

Of course. Mrs. Brooks was a photographer.

I glanced back at him to see his dark hair was messy like he had been nervously running his hands through it as I had wandered through his personal space, making my assessment. Did this make him nervous, I wondered? Me invading his privacy, staring at his things? Maybe he had secrets. The thought stirred my inner villain.

"It's amazing." I meant it. To say anything else would be pointless. He'd know I was lying.

His eyes met mine for a moment, rounding in surprise. Then the flicker of light from a car passing outside slid across the ceiling, drawing my eye. I glanced to it and gasped. It had been painted to look like his room was underwater. Somehow the artist had perfectly captured the pale shade of blue and the rippling surface, along with the way sunlight bounced off the cool water during the summer.

"Incredible, right?" he asked, and I could hear the smile in his voice.

"Who did it?"

"The same artist who did the ship on the plaque over our garage."

"It's awesome."

"The only thing that sucks about it is that I

can't take it with me next year."

Ah, yes, next year. The painful reminder settled in my chest. "The only thing I wish I could take with me from home is Ethan. If I could pack him up in my bags, I would."

Carson was silent for so long, I glanced at him to make sure he was still breathing. Unfortunately, he was.

"Right. Because my little brother's so amazing," he muttered, and I detected something bitter in his tone.

"Jealous much?"

His cheeks flushed, and I wondered if it was from embarrassment or anger. "You guys spend a lot of time together is all."

"He's my best friend."

Carson shook his head and moved to his bed, where he flopped down, then threaded his hands behind his neck. "Which is weird."

"How is that weird?" First my father and now him.

Carson shrugged. "I don't know. It just is. You're the only girl I know who's *that* close to a guy she's not interested in dating."

His eyes drifted to mine, then away again.

"I suppose you got a free ride to some amazing school," I said, changing the subject.

"Swimming is my ticket."

"Your ticket?" I asked.

"Out of Sweet Water. Maybe to the Olympics," he added. "One can dream. You and Ethan have the grades. I have swimming."

"The next Michael Phelps."

Carson scoffed. "If only..."

It really wasn't far off. I could totally see a load of gold medals decorating his neck one day. Of course, I didn't say that. No need to inflate his ego to mega proportions.

I sauntered over to the chair at his desk and took a seat. "When did you get an offer?" I asked.

"Offers," he clarified. "Last year. It's official now though."

"Where to? Please tell me it's in another country." I needed to calculate the distance from Durham to wherever he'd be. If he said it was on the West Coast, I would cry tears of joy.

"Duke."

The blood drained from my face.

No, he was kidding. He heard my conversation with Ethan, and he was teasing me. Surely...

I blinked at him for a moment, waiting for him to crack a smile, to laugh—something. But he didn't. He was serious. As I looked closer, I noted the hint of excitement in his eyes, the anticipation, the pride.

Oh my gosh…

"What about you? Where are you going?" he asked, and I wanted to sob.

Wherever will accept me, I wanted to say, but I stopped myself. I sighed and tucked a lock of hair behind my ear. "I'm not sure yet. I applied for early admission to a handful of places but haven't heard back. I should know something soon."

"Okay, so where's your number one, then?"

I gathered the cuffs of my hoodie in the palms of my hands, squirming. Should I lie? Knowing Carson, he would say I wanted Duke because of him, if for no other reason than to irritate me.

"Uh, Duke, actually," I muttered.

Carson sat up. "For real?"

I barked out a laugh. "I kid you not."

He stared at me a moment before a smile snaked over his features. "I knew you'd miss me next year. Couldn't stay away, Shorty?"

I scoffed. "You wish. In fact, now that I know that's where you're going, I'm reevaluating all my life choices. I'm thinking Sweet Water Community College sounds pretty good right about now."

"Right. Like you're not secretly filled with joy at the thought." He leaned back on his elbows, his shirt tightening over his chest.

"More like dread."

Carson chuckled. "I'm surprised. I took you as a lifer like Ethan."

"No, I need out of here." The words spilled out of my mouth before I could stop them.

Crap. That one sentence revealed too much.

Carson's brow creased, and I glanced away, adding, "I'm surprised by you though. For someone who loves to swim and loves the beach as much as you do, I would've thought you'd want to stay right here in Sweet Water."

"Eh. You can swim anywhere, and Duke has an amazing swim program, unlike the colleges nearby. Plus, there happens to be an ex-Olympian there who wants to work with me. I love it here, and Sweet Water will always be home, but I want to try new things, new places. I need something to keep me on my toes. Sweet Water is just so…"

"Limiting," we said in unison.

Our eyes locked, and my stomach dipped. Clearing my throat, I said, "Anyway, we should probably get started."

From the corner of my eye, I noticed his small frown before it disappeared. "Okay, I'm ready. Hit me with it. How much work is it?"

I rummaged through my bag, retrieving the folder, then opened it and spread the contents out on Carson's desk. "So, I went through everything

Mrs. Parks gave us, then I also did a little planning." I took out the spreadsheets I made with our divided tasks and stood, handing it to him.

"I think if we put our minds to it, we can knock out a lot of the work this weekend and be done in a week or so with only delivery left and minimal interaction on our part."

He grunted at the spreadsheet. "I don't know if that works for me."

"Well, I just thought we could divide and conquer." *Since we can't stand each other.* "I figured it might go. . .uh. . .more smoothly. I made a list. So, if you want to see if there's anything you think we should add," I said, motioning toward the paper, "now's the time."

He stood and moved next to me, peering down at the spreadsheet from over my shoulder. He was a giant with me sitting below him, and I squirmed in his proximity. I could practically feel him breathing down my neck from above.

"If we get the tree up this weekend and rake in some more donors, then all we'll have left to do is the shopping and delivery," I said.

"There's only one problem with all of this."

"What?" I blinked up at him.

"I have meets all day Saturday, and then Sunday we have—"

"Carson, I can't wait for you to be free. I

mean, I realize swimming is important, and you have a social life, but this is important, too. It's either we complete this, or we take the suspension, which from the sounds of things, isn't a viable option for either of us if I want to gain early admission and you want to keep your scholarship."

He raked a hand through his hair. "I get that. And I realize that my schedule makes things difficult, but it is what it is."

It is what it is? Why was he always so cavalier about everything? It was super annoying. Maybe the most annoying thing about him on a long, long list.

"I'll handle it," I said, standing and walking to the bed, where I scooped up the spreadsheet I handed him. "I'll just do it all. It'll be easier that way."

"Whoa. Wait a minute." He grabbed my wrist, stopping me, then yanked the paper out of my hands. "We're supposed to do this together, remember? Or has your little bump to the head made you forget."

My nostrils flared, and his eyes hardened on my face, unapologetic, but I stood my ground. No way would I give him the upper hand.

Realizing his hand was still around my wrist, I shook him off and pointed at him. "I heard what she said, and I know what peer mediation is, thank you very much, but seeing as how you have no time to spare—"

"I'll make the time." The muscle in his jaw flexed.

I wanted to say no. To refuse. But I could hardly do that, could I? As much as I hated to admit it, he was right. We were supposed to work on this together, that was the whole point, and if we didn't comply, Mrs. Parks would have no choice but to suspend us.

"Fine. Sunday, then. After whatever thing you have going on."

"Fine." He crossed his arms over his chest, taking a defiant stance, and I wanted to tell him to stop because it only made his shoulders look broader, his arms bigger. Blech.

I cocked my hip, shifting my gaze. "We'll start with putting the tree up Sunday then go from there. Sound good?"

"How's four o'clock work? You may as well come to dinner after. Ethan will want you to, and my parents adore you." He rolled his eyes. "Though I don't know why."

I smiled tightly, but inside, I was thrilled at the prospect of another peaceful meal away from home. "They love me because I'm the daughter they wish they had instead of their firstborn." I turned from him and said, "Now, let's go over this list."

CHAPTER FIVE

I flipped the visor mirror back up and turned to Ethan. "Okay, so my eye still isn't great despite my epic concealer blending skills and the translucent powder I used."

Ethan raised a brow. "I don't know what you just said, but it's not that bad. There's just a little bruising. Don't be so self-conscious."

"Easy for you to say," I grumbled, because when you grew up with hair the color of sun-ripened peaches and skin as white as snow, you kind of had a complex about your looks.

"No one will even say anything about it. It's old news. Remember that time Kent and Brian got in that fight last year over Lori? It was over the next day."

I exhaled. "You're right." I nodded and chewed on my lower lip before getting out of the car and following Ethan inside.

What was I so afraid of, anyway? It was no secret Carson and I were rivals. Who cared if people heard I finally snapped and went after him? It shouldn't be a surprise. If anything, I deserved an award for putting up with his torment all these years. I was practically a saint.

Ethan said goodbye and headed for his locker shortly after we walked through the door, leaving me alone.

I received a couple raised brows. Or maybe I was just paranoid.

When I got to my locker, I quickly entered the combination, popped the lock, and put my things inside.

I grabbed the books I needed for the first couple classes, then slammed the door shut and spun around, but not before Carl Macky stopped across from me and put his hands up by his face and flinched. "No. Don't hurt me. Please." He fake-cowered.

Confused, I glanced around, but the only kids nearby were his friends and a couple random spectators. And then it clicked.

He moved his hands in front of his throat

and told the guy next to him. "Protect yourself. Randalls is lethal."

They were making fun of me. Great. Even though I had expected this to happen, it still made my stomach clench and my palms sweat. I laughed like I actually thought he was funny instead of the total jerk he was and rolled my eyes, playing it off. "Good one."

Carl chuckled and high-fived his friends like he accomplished something worth celebrating then sauntered off.

I guess ten seconds was enough to get his kicks.

I lifted my hair up into a ponytail with my hands, wondering if it was a waste of time to curl it into soft waves if all people were going to do was focus on my face, then I let it drop and fall over my shoulders. "It'll be okay, Mia," I murmured to myself. "Just get through the day."

With a sigh, I pushed off my lockers, then headed to class, where I had trouble following along. Instead of discussing the relevance of *A Tale Of Two Cities* in today's modern world, I was silently dreading the rest of the day and the weekend because Sunday meant spending more time with Carson.

After this week, there was only one week of school left before we'd be out for winter break. One week left to find a date to the dance. With a swollen eye and my newfound reputation for strangling my classmates.

Unlike Katniss Everdeen from The Hunger Games, the odds were not in my favor. There was no way I was coming out of the gauntlet with a date now, which was disappointing. In only four months, I'd graduate, which meant preparing to leave for college. I had wanted one final year of making as many memories as I could with my friends—with Ethan.

By the time I entered my fifth-period Chemistry class, I had thought I was in the clear. Other than Macky in the hall this morning, no one said much about my feud with Carson. Unfortunately, he was in my chemistry class, so there was no avoiding him.

When I entered the room, I took my seat at the large lab table next to my partner, Sarah, while avoiding eye-contact with the table next to ours where I knew Carson would be seated. A ripple of excitement swept through the room as a substitute entered. Once we were given our lab assignment, each table got to work collecting beakers, PH test strips, scales, and everything else we required for the experiment. After making sure I had everything, I returned to my lab table with the last of our things, and Sarah yawned, then said, "Oh my gosh. I got no sleep last night. I'm just spent."

I said nothing, knowing where this was going because if there was one way in which I could rely on Sarah as a partner, it was for her to be epically lazy. More often than not, she copied my notes and homework. Rarely did she actually help me with any of the labs or experiments, and the fact that we had a sub made it exponentially easier for her to slack off.

"Do you think you could handle this one? Maybe I could just watch and take notes," she said, though we both knew her idea of taking notes was napping behind her bookbag.

I sighed. For once, I wanted to say no. I wanted to tell her I was sick of pulling her weight.

Movement from a table over caught my eye, and when I looked, I saw Carson arch a brow, nodding toward Sarah. Then he pulled a face and made a slashing movement across his throat as if to tell me not to do it.

Turning back to her, I opened my mouth to tell her no, but what came out was, "Whatever."

Out of the corner of my eye, Carson shook his head, disappointed, which annoyed me. It's not like it was him doing the extra work. What did he care?

Before I could even shoot him a dirty look, he was raising his hand and asking, "Uh, my partner's out sick today. Do you care if I pair up with another group?" The substitute waved him off and nodded, more interested in his magazine than anything happening in the classroom, and before I could protest, Carson was brushing Sarah aside and bumping into me.

"What are you doing?" I asked, feigning annoyance. Even if the world were ending, I would never admit that deep down, I was actually kind of glad to have a real partner. Even if it was Carson.

"You're welcome." He grinned.

I placed one hand on my hip. "Like I need your help."

"At least you won't have to do all the work alone," Carson said. "And if there's one thing I'm good at, Shorty, it's chemistry." He wiggled his brows, earning him an eye roll.

Behind us, we heard a couple of kids snicker, followed by a wad of paper whacking me in the back. Turning, I glanced around the room, but everyone was laser-focused on their experiment, all eyes on their table, except for Tasha who met my gaze quickly before glancing away again.

Frowning, I unraveled the ball of paper. Inside was a rather crude rendition of a girl strangling someone. I had no doubts about who the two people were supposed to be.

From over my shoulder, Carson snatched the paper away. I expected him to laugh, but instead, he whipped around to the sound of Tasha and her partner's laughter and barked out, "Knock it off, guys." Then he strode over to the trash can and threw it inside.

When he returned, I avoided his eye. "Um, thanks."

"People haven't been bugging you about that, have they?"

"No," I lied, mostly because other than Tasha's rather defunct art skills, Macky was the only one to pick on me and being mean was just a part of who he was.

"Good," he said. "Because if they were, they'd have to answer to me."

Then he pointed to our lab sheets and started on our experiment.

School on Friday was uneventful, thank goodness. No one said anything else about the gym incident, and only a few people commented on my eye. The rest probably had already chalked it up to just another fight between us. After all, it was no secret we were enemies.

I spent most of the weekend hanging out with Ethan. Sunday was no exception, and we spent the majority of it lazing about in his room since the weather was cold and rainy. At the moment, I was currently lounging on his bedroom floor, staring up at the ceiling, thinking of how much cooler Carson's room was compared to his— not that I would ever tell Ethan that.

I groaned and shook more chips from the bag into my bowl. "I don't want tomorrow to be Monday."

"Why? You have a killer test or something?" Ethan asked, taking a handful of chips.

"No. I promised Mrs. Parks I'd come to school early so I could show a newb around the school." And if tomorrow's Monday, that meant today was Sunday, and the time I'd have to spend with Carson was fast approaching.

"Oh." Ethan wiggled his brows. "New guy?"

"Uh, no. It's a freshman and a girl," I said.

Ethan grunted. "Why are you always helping her out, anyway? It's not like you get anything out of it. Plus, she punished you. Shouldn't you hate her and be retaliating or something?"

"No," I said, not meeting his eye. "I help because she asked, and I don't want her to be mad at me."

"It's Mrs. Parks. She's always mad at everyone. It's her job."

Not me, I wanted to say.

"You don't always have to do what makes everyone else happy, you know. Sometimes you can say no. Do what you want."

I kept my head down, intently staring at my chips.

"Mia," Ethan said, "look at me."

"What?" I shrugged, trying to look innocent. "Listen, I don't need one of your lectures, okay? It's fine. I'm fine. It gets me out of the house, anyway."

Ethan sighed, grumbling something under his breath about being a people pleaser that I chose to ignore. So what if I wanted people to like me. Was that such a crime?

I glanced at my watch and moaned. It was almost noon, which meant I'd soon have to leave for The Bean to set up the Angel Tree. Every time I thought about having to spend time with Carson again one-on-one, my stomach twisted. But I wasn't nervous. I was anxious. Big difference.

"I can't believe Carson and I survived our lab on Thursday without killing each other. You know, there was even a moment there where I thought we were getting along, which reminds me," I rolled from my back onto my stomach and narrowed my eyes at him. "Why didn't you tell me he was going to Duke? You know that's my number one."

Ethan sunk down beside me on the floor, propping himself up against the footboard of his bed. "I was going to tell you at dinner Wednesday night when we were loading the dishwasher, and then I thought, why ruin it for you? You need to go where you want, without anything or anyone influencing you. That, and I didn't want to be the bearer of bad news." He laughed.

I screwed up my face. I guess he had a point. "You're forgiven, even though you have a hot date to the dance, and I do not."

"You're going to the dance. Someone will ask you. You have two weeks yet."

I raised a brow. Wow. Two whole weeks. "Even after choking a guy out in front of my entire gym class? Yeah, I'm sure all the guys are just dying to ask me out. In fact, they're probably fighting over me now, which is why no one's asked yet." I rolled my eyes. "Friday at lunch, I saw Tasha and Olivia huddled together with a couple other MG's, miming strangling themselves at the lunch table. And their eyes definitely met mine afterward. None of the boys in my class are going to want to touch me with a ten-foot pole."

Ethan pursed his lips, then shrugged. "You have a point."

I threw a chip at him, but he darted forward and caught it in his mouth.

"Impressive. I can't even be mad now." I laughed.

"Sorry I can't go to the dance with you," he said, and I shrugged.

"It's not your fault you have a girl you like who actually likes you back." At his glare, I corrected. "Okay, I know. I don't even like anyone, and it's not like I'm really trying, but still…"

"Why *don't* you like anyone?"

I took a sip of my soda to buy me time. "Do I have to?"

"It's just, you haven't been interested in anyone since sophomore year. What's up with that?"

"I don't know. I guess…" I set the chips in my hand back in the bowl and wiped my hands on a napkin, sitting up. "Things are so serious at home that it hasn't been my focus."

"But going out, dating, it would be good for you, a distraction."

"I'm not arguing. But I've been busting my butt to smash the SAT's and get good grades so that I get into the college of my choice. Most of my energy is going into that. There's not much left to spare. That, and I guess no one has caught my eye."

"No one?"

I frowned. "What's with all the questions? You and I never talk about my love life or lack thereof. You always tell me you want no part of it. That it's gross."

Ethan crammed a potato chip in his mouth. "No reason."

I bit the inside of my cheek. I knew when he was lying. There was most definitely a reason he was asking. But I'd let it go for now.

He swallowed, then asked, "Do you think if you actually liked me our parents would let you hang in my room all the time?"

"Uh, no. Definitely not. Although it's not like my parents are paying much attention to anything I do these days."

"That would suck."

I nodded my agreement and grinned. "You better keep all those feelings you harbor for me deep down to yourself, so I don't get banned." I wiggled my eyebrows and he laughed.

CHAPTER SIX

I popped into The Bean at precisely three thirty. The aroma of freshly roasted coffee beans hit me as I approached the counter and took a cursory glance around the small coffee shop. I didn't see Carson anywhere. He mustn't have arrived yet, and I hoped he wouldn't be late since it was a Sunday and they closed early. I had agreed to meet him since he was finishing up some kind of swim team gathering. With a lot of foot traffic year-round, The Bean was the perfect location for the Angel Tree. It would get the most exposure there, and I wasn't hating the idea of working on it inside the confines of the little coffee shop. It was warm and cozy with its neutral color scheme, ambient lighting, and the nutty aroma of their on-site roasted java. Not to mention, I didn't hate the excuse to enjoy a gingerbread latte.

Maddie was working the counter, handing a customer their change and a cup of coffee as I walked up. I put my hand up in a little wave.

"Hey, girl," Maddie said. "What's up?"

"Nothing. Just meeting someone here," I said, unsure of why I was being evasive. It's not like she wasn't going to see me with him.

"*Oh*, who's the boy? Is he cute? Someone from school?" Maddie's eyes glittered with interest.

I chuckled at her enthusiasm. "I don't know. Cute is in the eye of the beholder, I suppose. It's Carson Brooks."

"Definitely not cute then, because he's a total hottie."

Was he hot? I supposed if you considered annoying boys with broad shoulders and muscular arms hot.

An image of him as we stood toe-to-toe on his porch flickered in my head, and my cheeks caught fire as I remembered the way his long-sleeved shirt clung to his chest. I bet his abs were hard as concrete from all that swimming.

Did I really just think that?

I grunted a noncommittal response, then

ordered a gingerbread latte. As Maddie got to work on my drink, she glanced up at me from behind the espresso machine. "Are you guys working on the Angel Tree thing?"

I groaned. "You heard about that, too?"

"Has anyone not heard about that?" She laughed and flicked her long hair out of her face.

"I'm going down as the crazy girl who tried to choke someone, aren't I?"

"In truth? Most of the girls, except for the MG's, think it was pretty awesome. I mean, the boy pummeled you with the ball and you fought back. It was savage. Now, the boys, on the other hand. . ." She trailed off as she scrunched her nose.

Great. "Fabulous. Because I totally wanted to be single my entire senior year," I said, taking my coffee from her.

There was time for dating in college, I mused. New school. New boys.

What was I saying? They wouldn't *all* be new boys. Carson and I may be going to the same school. How weird was that?

I took a hesitant sip of my latte, careful not to burn myself as the chimes on the door behind me rang. I turned just in time to see Carson stroll inside like he owned the place. When his gaze caught mine, he gave me a head nod, before saying hi to Maddie.

"See? So hot," Maddie muttered under her breath, and I glanced back at her with a frown.

When Carson stopped beside me, he shoved his hands in his pockets and asked, "You ready?"

"Don't you want coffee?" Maddie asked. "I can make you something extra sweet," she drawled.

I blinked over at her, amazed at her transformation from friendly to vixen. She leaned over the counter, ample cleavage on full display as she fluttered her lashes.

But either Carson didn't notice, or he wasn't interested because his eyes never left me as he reached out and snatched my cup from my grasp, then took a sip.

"Hey!" I shouted and reached for it. "Now it's got your germs on it." My lip curled in disgust as he handed it back to me and winked.

I ignored the flush of heat in my cheeks as I took the sleeve of my sweater and exaggeratedly wiped the lid of my cup off as I shot daggers at him with my eyes. Unfazed, he pointed to it and said, "I'll take whatever that is."

"It's a gingerbread latte," I muttered.

"Whatever."

While Maddie got to work on his drink, I felt her eyes on us, so I shifted further away from the counter, shrinking under her gaze. "Did you get the tree from school on Friday?" I asked him.

"Yup."

"Great. I brought the snowflakes to write on and the permanent markers."

Carson nodded, but he didn't seem all that interested. His eyes scanned my face, lingering on the area around my eye, the one he whacked with the ball. The purple had turned to a mottled yellow-brown color in the last day. It wasn't exactly attractive, but it was fading at least. Plus, the swelling was gone. My fear of living the rest of my days as a cyclops had abated.

He reached out and gently brushed the bruised skin with a finger, his touch featherlight, turning my stomach into knots. "Your eye's a little better."

My skin burned in the wake of his fingertips. "Um, yeah. It's getting there."

He swallowed, then he ruffled his dark hair with his hands before forcefully shoving them into his pockets. *Was it me or did he seem. . .nervous?*

When Maddie called his name, I tore my gaze from his as she slid his coffee across the counter toward him, a smug grin curling the corners of her lips. He took it hastily, fidgeting with the plastic lid, and the moment his back was turned to Maddie again, she mouthed *He likes you.*

What? *No*, I mouthed back, then rolled my eyes because, *sure, he does.* Carson Brooks and I were the human equivalents of oil and water. He liked me about as much as an older brother cherished his annoying kid-sister.

But she simply widened her eyes in response to my eye roll as if I was crazy. After, she waved us away, and I awkwardly took that as my cue and pulled Carson along. "Why don't you go get the tree, and then we'll get started," I said.

Fifteen minutes later, the artificial pine was up in the corner of the coffee shop, away from the front door but visible to anyone coming and going. Carson and I sat across from each other at one of The Bean's little bistro tables, our lattes all but gone, the remaining supplies splayed out in front of us.

"Here are the requests," I said, handing him his half of the spreadsheet. "They have names on them and the gift to be purchased. We have to write them both on the snowflakes. These are for the gifts for the children's hospital and the Sweet Water nursing home. The other stuff we have to do is for the Sweet Water Christmas Angel Program where they adopt a handful of families, so that's separate."

"So community members buy the items on the snowflakes, and we seek out donors for the adopted families and make those purchases. Am I right?" Carson asked.

He was taking this seriously, which surprised me. "Exactly. Plus, we buy and organize the holiday food baskets for them, too, and purchase any items that go unclaimed on the tree. So, really, it's kind of two programs we're working on, not one."

"And Mrs. Parks thought she'd pawn it all off on us. Nice."

I laughed. "Exactly."

"I guess we had it coming though." He smiled, and I wondered if he recalled the moment I stormed across the gym and tried to throttle him or the one where he whacked me in the face with the basketball.

I cocked my head. "So you admit you hit me intentionally?"

"Intentionally is a strong word. Maybe I sort of aimed it your way. You were talking to Harper, and you looked all doom and gloom. What was that about, anyway?"

"Oh, so you thought, *Mia looks sad. Let's hit her in the face with a ball*?" I said, ignoring his question. "Wow. That's some interesting problem-solving skills you got there. Way to make a girl feel better about herself by giving her a black eye. Now I see why you're single."

"Ouch. That might hurt if you weren't single, too."

Gee, thanks for pointing out the obvious. I screwed up my face, and he laughed. "I just meant to hit you—I don't know—in the back or the side or something, but you guys stopped walking the moment I threw it. Plus, you bruise easily. How was I supposed to know?" He shrugged, leaning back in his chair. "I just thought that if I could make you angry, then you wouldn't be sad or upset or whatever."

I swallowed. Why did that sound kind of sweet? Carson was never sweet. At least not to me.

I opened my mouth to respond when the door chimed and the unmistakable high-pitched voice of Olivia called out, "Hey, Carson."

Ugh.

Carson's gaze lifted from mine toward the source of the sound, and he smiled, which made my stomach sink—and not in a good way. I didn't want him smiling at her, which was more alarming than any thought I'd had all day.

"What's up?" he answered.

I swiveled around in my chair to get a glimpse of the intruder. Her blonde hair was pulled up into a sleek ponytail. She wore skinny jeans that could rival a second skin and three-inch heels, with an itty-biddy sweater that was one arm-reach away from exposing her navel. By her side was Tasha.

Great. The double threat.

"Oh, hi, Mia. I didn't see you there."

Was I invisible now? I was sitting right there.

"Yeah." I lamely waved a paper snowflake in the air. "We're working on...stuff," I mumbled because it was evident by her expression she wasn't interested. Her gaze had zeroed in on Carson and she wasn't leaving his sight.

Everything inside me willed Olivia and Tasha to the coffee counter, to order their double-skinny-chai-almond-milk-sugar free-whatever's and go, but instead, they closed in on our table.

My life was awesome.

Olivia paused and rested her hand on the table in front of me like I wasn't even there, while Tasha scrolled through her phone. She probably thought she was too good to even be standing in my presence.

"So, Carson, I heard you don't have a date for the Snowflake Ball yet."

My eyes widened and every muscle in my body stiffened at her mention of the dance. Carson must've noticed the shift in demeanor because his brow furrowed as he glanced at me out of the corner of his eye, then back to Olivia.

I pulled my hands under the table and clasped them in prayer. *Please don't let her bring up her conversation with me. Please.* If she told him she asked me to mention the dance to him—which I didn't—he might think it was because I didn't want him to take her or worse, because I liked him. That couldn't be the furthest thing from the truth. I just forgot. I've had a lot on my mind.

"Nope." He clasped his hands behind his head, reclining in his seat. "I'm waiting, exploring my options," he said evasively.

I snorted. *Must be nice.*

"Yeah, I'm not sure who I'm going with yet either," Olivia purred. "I'll have to see if anyone else asks." She pursed her overly glossed lips, and I wanted to groan. Instead, I took a sip of my latte, thinking, *could you be more obvious?!*

"Aren't you going with Steve? I'm pretty sure that's what he told me."

Olivia's face fell as coffee entered my wind-pipe, and I started coughing like an idiot, trying to hack it up.

"Sorry," I muttered between gasps for air, then bumped Carson's cup in the process, spilling the rest of his drink.

Crap. I hurried with the napkins, reaching over the table, mopping up the gingerbread coffee. Half-standing, I began to dab at Carson's lap before

I realized what I was doing and froze. The palm of my hand scorched as his eyes caught mine, the blue blazing.

I wrenched my arm back so fast I almost tore it from the socket. Wincing, I noticed Olivia's glare. Biting my lip, I tentatively glanced up at her, and from what I gleaned in her expression, she was not amused.

"That's funny," Olivia said. "Because I saw Mia on her way to your place just the other night and I specifically told her I didn't have an official date yet. *And* I asked her to see if maybe you were still looking. Because if you are, I'd be interested." She pouted her lips and turned her flirtatious gaze back to Carson, and I wanted to puke.

But Carson just smiled and said, "I didn't know Mia was your messenger."

I couldn't tell if he was flirting or annoyed. Weirdly enough, it almost sounded like he was sticking up for me. Either way, Olivia giggled and touched his arm.

"Well, now you know," she said.

"I will take it under advisement," Carson said, his smile tight.

"Great. You do that." Olivia clicked her acrylic fingernails on the table, then with a wink, she turned to where Tasha was impatiently waiting off to the side, and they headed to the counter.

When I finally shoved down my annoyance enough to look at him, I realized he'd been watching me. "What?" I asked, noting the question in his eyes.

"Nothing," he said, but the lilt to his voice told me it wasn't nothing.

I frowned and threw a sugar packet at him. "What?"

"I just find it interesting that you didn't want to tell me about your encounter with Olivia."

"Ugh. I knew you'd think I had some ulterior reason for not telling you, but the truth is I just forgot."

"Forgot." He said the word like he was trying to decipher the meaning. "Was this Wednesday when you came over to discuss the project?"

"Yeah." I shrugged. What was his point?

"That's interesting. Because I saw you outside before you even entered the house which means you had probably just run into Olivia. It's amazing how you forgot so quickly. Like within minutes."

I scoffed. "You have a way about you that makes me instantly forget everything." My cheeks burned as the words left my lips, knowing how they would sound. That totally wasn't what I meant.

"Really?" He raised his brows, and sure enough, he was running with it. "My presence is so intoxicating it makes your brain shut down? I mean, I knew I had that power over other girls, but not you."

"That's not what I meant." I gripped my cup so hard, I thought it might burst. "I *meant* that you annoy me. You're so infuriating that I forget."

"Uh-huh, sure. Whatever you say."

"I'm serious."

"I know. Sure, you are." His stupid blue eyes sparkled as he teased.

"See. Right now is a perfect example," I said through gritted teeth.

He laughed, to which I growled and subsequently grabbed my first snowflake and angrily scribbled the first name and gift on it. He took his first one and did the same, smug smile still in place.

After a few minutes, I forgot how annoyed I was, wrapped up in the requests on the page, the simple wants and desires from people who had very little. Things we took for granted like body wash, a shaving kit, lotion, fuzzy socks, and slippers. Once we finished, we began hanging them on the tree with string.

"Are you going to the dance?" Carson asked, breaking the silence.

His question surprised me. Was he still thinking about that?

"Um. I don't know. I mean, it's our last winter formal, so I'd like to," I said, conveniently leaving out the part where I didn't have a date.

"Who's taking you?" He turned to the tree, but I could see him glancing my way out of the corner of his eye.

"Uh, what?"

"I asked who you're going with?"

"I think we need to spread these out a little more," I said, motioning toward a cluster of snow-flakes.

"Why are you avoiding my question?"

"I'm not avoiding your question."

"You totally are."

"Am not."

He placed his hands on his hips. "Then why haven't you answered me yet?"

"Because I don't have a date. Happy?"

Carson grinned. "Kind of."

I glared at him, wondering if I could melt him with my eyes. When I didn't say anything else, he asked, "So, little Miss Perfect is dateless, huh?"

"Shuddup."

"How could you not have a date? Did no one

ask you, or did you turn them all down?"

Turn them all down. Funny guy.

I weighed my options. Tell him the truth or lie. Lying would save face, but if he somehow found out I was lying, then I'd look like an even bigger loser.

Clearing my throat, I settled on the truth. "At first, I thought Ethan and I might go, but then he wanted to ask someone, and the next thing I knew it was getting closer, and now...Maddie said I scared off all the guys at school with the gym class incident."

"Nah. That's not true."

I flashed him a look that said he was wrong —Carl Macky came to mind.

"Seriously. I'm a guy. Shouldn't I know?" he asked.

"Well, the guys certainly weren't beating my door down before. I highly doubt they will be now."

"That doesn't mean they don't want to. You're unattainable."

"Little Miss Perfect, I know." I sneered.

He shook his head. "No, that's not what I meant."

I paused, a snowflake in my hand, and looked at him like he was crazy. "What are you talking about?"

"You. You're that girl at school that's hard to catch. A lot of guys are just too afraid to try and get shot down."

I shook my head. "No way. That's ridiculous."

"Is it? You have one of the highest GPA's in our class, you were class president two years in a row, not to mention, involved in a lot of extra-curriculars, you're sweet to everyone, even the MG's," he whispered as Olivia and Tasha took a seat a few tables down. "And it totally shows because everyone likes you."

"I'm not friends with everyone—"

"You are, Mia. The geeks, the jocks, the surfers, the mean girls, the potheads, you name the group and they all like you. And I might be a dude, but even I know the fact that Tasha and Olivia even acknowledge you says something. They can be downright brutal to the other chicks." He placed his snowflake on the tree then grabbed another. "Trust me. Guys want to ask, but when it comes down to it, they're too afraid. But not for the reasons you think."

"I'm not friends with you," I said simply because I had to prove a point.

Carson grunted, avoiding my eye and hung another snowflake, but all I could do was stare at him, partly in shock, partially assessing his level of serious. Because either I was going insane or Carson Brooks just gave me the most epic of compliments.

CHAPTER SEVEN

Monday morning, I slammed my locker door closed when Lauren Carmichael sidled up next to me. Her blonde ponytail bobbing, eyes bright. "How was your time spent with Carson this weekend? Maddie told Jenna she saw you guys at The Bean."

Why did news always have to spread so fast at Sweet Water? And since when was I the subject aboard the gossip train?

Oh, yeah. Probably since I tried to strangle a boy in gym class.

"Torturous," I answered.

Lauren's smile fell, and I laughed. "What? You look disappointed."

She shrugged. "It's just you guys have more chemistry than Mr. Catson's science experiments."

"Are you sure *you* weren't the one who was hit in the head last week?"

Ethan exited his classroom and caught sight of us, following behind as we headed toward the cafeteria.

"I'm serious. It's true," Lauren said. "Tell her, Ethan. You're his brother. You've got to see it, too."

"See what?" Ethan raised a brow and glanced over at me while I tried my best to keep my expression neutral.

"Lauren has some crazy idea that Carson and I. . ." I nearly gagged on the word as I choked out, "Have chemistry."

Ethan wrinkled his nose. "With Carson? I guess if you consider eternal hatred chemistry, then. . ."

"Exactly." I grinned, thanking him with my smile.

"Ugh. Whatever," Lauren said. "Are you guys going to his party on Saturday night? Wes and I already have plans or we'd be there."

Ethan groaned. "He's having another party? I totally should've known since my parents are going out of town for their anniversary."

"We never go to his parties," I added.

"Why not? They're fun."

"You think they're fun because you guys run cross-country with him, and because, in the smallest of ways, you have him to thank for you and Wes hooking up."

When Lauren blushed, I smiled. "Or are the rumors wrong?"

Ignoring me, Lauren turned to Ethan. "But you're his brother. I never get why you're not there."

Ethan paused with us outside the cafeteria, which was his cue to head to History class and ours to lunch. "It's simple. If I don't know what he's doing when my parents aren't home, then I can't tell and don't have to lie when I'm asked. It makes life easier."

"And you?" Lauren asked me. "What's your excuse?"

"For one, I'm usually hanging with Ethan. Like I want to go to Carson's party so he can make it his night's mission to irritate me to death. With my luck, he'd probably dare me to go for a midnight swim at the beach in one of his rousing games of truth or dare and I'd drown. Besides, he's never actually invited me to one of his parties. Isn't an invitation sort of a prerequisite? Showing up would make me look desperate." Or like I cared.

Truth be told, I'd always been a little intrigued by Carson's epic parties. If he wielded the kind of power that could help nudge Lauren and Wes out of their giant family feud, then I was interested to see it firsthand. Call it curiosity.

"Fine. But you two are missing out," Lauren said, pointing between us. "And just so you know," she whispered so only I could hear. "I heard Olivia's on the prowl, and she plans on crashing."

I sat in study hall, notes spread out in front of me, prepping for the big calculus test before winter break when someone tapped me on the shoulder and handed me a tiny piece of notebook paper. The paper was folded into an origami star. Frowning, I glanced around me to see who the sender was. I knew it wasn't Emmy Banks who sat to my right because my name on the front was written in what was most definitely a boy's handwriting.

Glancing around the room for the culprit, my gaze slid over my classmates until they locked on Carson's and he winked. My stomach clenched as I turned back around and slowly opened the note, wondering what he wanted that couldn't wait until after class. *"Want to meet up after school to discuss the donors and when we might want to go shopping?"*

Of course it was about the Angel Project. What was I expecting?

I grabbed my pencil and scribbled, "Sure." Then I handed the note back to Ky behind me, who passed it to Lucas, then back to Carson. I saw him unfold it out of the corner of my eye, then smile and write something else.

When I got the note back, I opened it up, more eager than I'd like to admit. *"Great. Meet me at The Bread Basket after school, 3:00."*

I entered The Bread Basket at five 'till three, wondering why Carson chose that particular location. Not that I didn't like baked goods, but it seemed like a strange meeting place. However, the moment I entered and saw him leaning against the counter talking to Winny, the owner, I overheard their conversation, and it clicked.

His attention turned to me. "Hey." He hooked a thumb toward Winny and said, "The Bread Basket is donating dinner rolls, bread, and cinnamon rolls for the holiday food baskets. Enough for each family to eat on Christmas and have leftovers to freeze."

For a moment, I was speechless. I hadn't even thought to ask local businesses for nonmonetary donations. The fact that Carson had said a lot.

"Wow. That's amazing, thanks Winny," I said, only slightly jealous I hadn't thought of it first.

"Oh, it's no problem. It's the least I can do to help. I think it's great you two are working on this project together. Not enough kids take the time to help people in need anymore. It's nice to see the youth of Sweet Water at work."

I smiled at her. She was too sweet for her own good. Obviously, Lucas hadn't told her the real reason we were stuck working on the project. If she only knew...

Carson, on the other hand, basked in the praise. "Well, thanks, but it's really our pleasure." He reached out and pulled me to his side, giving me a little shake like we were best buds. "Mia and I felt it was our duty to help our beloved town and its people in need, especially before we go off to school. It's the least we can do."

I jabbed him in the ribs when Winny glanced toward the sound of the door chimes.

"*Oomph.*" Carson winced before Winny turned back to us, and his plastic smile returned.

"Oh, where are you two going off to?" Whinny's eyes brightened.

"Duke," Carson answered before I could get a

word in.

I glared up at him, ignoring the way his goofy grin made my insides clench with. . .rage, I decided. It had to be.

"Both of you going to Duke? That's amazing. Congratulations."

"Yup. This time next year, we'll both be Blue Devils."

"Fitting for you," I mumbled under my breath, and Carson's smile broadened, his arm tightening around me.

"I'm sure your parents are proud."

At the mention of my parents, my heart skipped.

"We'll be sad to see you go, but I know you'll be back to visit," Winny continued.

"Absolutely," Carson said, then accepted the pledge Winny handed him.

Turning us around, he headed for the door. Once we got outside, a burst of cool air hit my face, and I seized the opportunity to wrench free from his arm. "Why? Why did you do that?" I spluttered.

"Do what?" he asked, his expression innocent.

"You told her I was going to Duke."

"Aren't you?"

I brought my hands to my temples and gently massaged away my blooming headache and groaned. "Yeah, sure. If I get in. I haven't received any early acceptance letters yet, let alone the one to Duke. Weren't you listening to me the other day?"

He shrugged. "Yeah, of course, I was. But you'll get in."

"You don't know that," I snapped. I stared him, jaw clenched, mouth set in a tight line. How was he always so casual about *everything*? Does nothing faze him? What must it be like to live in a world devoid of problems?

"It's not a big—"

"Yes, it is Carson. It is a big deal. A huge deal, actually. And if you knew even the slightest thing about me, you'd know that without me needing to tell you, but you don't. So just butt out."

"Mia. . ." He reached for my arm, but I side-stepped him, heading for my car.

"You know how Sweet Water is, and now everyone will know. Winny will tell Luca because she's happy for us, who will mention it to Charlotte, who will tell Maddie, who will tell every-freaking-one and then if I don't get in, I have to be the one to look like a fool and correct everybody. *Me!*" I stabbed myself in the chest. I could feel myself unraveling but was helpless to stop it. "While you're off in Durham chasing college girls, I'll be the loser who didn't get in."

Where did that come from?

Carson stared at me, his brow furrowed, concern in his eyes, and I wasn't sure what was worse, me feeling sorry for myself or him feeling sorry for me.

"Heck, my parents will even break out of their dysfunctional little bubble to catch wind of this piece of stellar news, and they'll be so excited," I continued, because why stop now? "This is news I've been dying to share with them. But I'll have to inform them that I don't know whether I got in or not yet and that it was just a rumor. Then I'll deal with the fallout. I'm sure it will turn into some massive fight between the two of them. My mother will blame my father for me not getting an acceptance letter yet, and he'll blame her for something else equally lame and out of her control. Then I'll just be some loser girl with no future, who tried to strangle a boy in gym class, and couldn't get a date to the dance, unless, of course, it was her best friend."

I gasped, taking a breath for the first time since I opened my mouth, and though everything I said was true, I realized it was probably a little overboard. My chest heaved with my emotions as I tried to reign them in, but they swirled slowly inside my chest, heavy like an anchor, threatening to drown me. I probably looked crazy. And though

I knew I shouldn't care—because this was Carson we were talking about—for some reason I couldn't pinpoint, I did care what he thought about me. A notion that made me even angrier.

"That was a lot to address all at once," Carson said, wide-eyed.

"Tell me about it," I rasped. Then I laughed, because, really, it was ironic. I poured out all my feelings to my nemesis.

"First of all, I know you more than you think, but if I don't, it's not because I don't want to. Maybe I want to know you better. Have you ever thought of that?"

I opened my mouth to interject because what he was saying was crazy, but he surprised me by placing his finger over my lips, silencing me before he continued, "Second, you *will* get in. Don't say you won't, or you don't know. Duke would be insane not to accept you. You're Mia-freaking-Randalls. Third, why on earth would your parents fight over whether you get into college or not?"

I groaned inwardly. This was not something I wanted to get into, especially with him of all people. I hardly even talked about it with Ethan, which was saying something.

"Nothing." I shook my head. "Forget I said anything. It's chilly out, can we just..."

I started to turn away and head for my car,

but Carson wrapped a hand around my arm and stopped me. "It's not nothing. I can see it in your eyes. This is what you were upset about the other day, wasn't it? College, your parents. . .what's going on, Mia?"

I wrapped my arms around myself, more out of comfort than to ward off the chill. "Like I would tell you."

Carson shoved his hands in his thick, dark hair, mussing it, as he paced in front of me. "Right. I forgot. I'm the jerk." He paused, staring at me with his aqua eyes. "You know, Ethan isn't the only one you can talk to. You can tell me things. I'd listen. I'd—"

I scoffed. "Did I miss something? Since when are we friends?"

Carson flinched, looking hurt, and part of me wanted to ask him where he'd been the last nine years. Since when did he and I get along? Just three weeks ago, Harper told me she overheard him telling Greg Thane I still sleep in Strawberry Shortcake PJ's, which was *totally* not true.

"I've always wanted to be your friend, Mia. It was never me turning you away."

I blinked up at him, my brow scrunched in confusion as I thought back to all our silly fights, his teasing, the antagonizing, and goading. Yes, Carson was every bit as much an equal player in our enemy-status. If anything, he was the instigator. So why was he trying to play it off now?

My confusion turned to a frown as I tried to wrap my head around the notion that he was insinuating he didn't hate me like I thought he did.

If I had learned one thing over the years, it was how lightly Carson took everything. While he was busy laughing at himself and the world around him, I was beating myself up, taking everything to heart. Maybe this whole time, I needed to take Carson at face value. He viewed life through rose-colored glasses, while I saw everything a little too clearly. And sometimes, when you got too close to things, magnified them too much, it distorted your view.

The trajectory of my thoughts was giving me a headache. I couldn't think about this now, so I cleared my throat and asked, "What other donors should we talk to today?"

I tried not to notice the disappointment in his eyes as he answered. "I figured we could go to the Sweet Water Market and see if they'd donate sandwich trays and ham. Those are expensive, so having them donated would allow us to spend the money elsewhere. The less we spend on food, the more toys and presents the kids can have under the tree."

"You've given this a lot of thought, haven't you?"

He shoved his hands in his pockets. "Everyone deserves a good Christmas."

"Yeah, they do." Then I thought of my depressing house with the fall décor still on display and the tension you could cut with a knife.

I shuddered out a long breath, then glanced up at him. The Carson standing in front of me, the one from chem lab and The Bean was different, not the boy I knew. "You surprise me," I said.

Carson laughed, and I warmed at the sound. "Maybe there's a lot you don't know about me."

Ever since The Bread Basket on Thursday, Carson and I had been friendly. *Weird, I know.*

He no longer plowed into me in the halls. I didn't find his stinky gym shoes in my locker or worry about flying objects in the cafeteria or at gym class. Yesterday after leaving calculus, he offered me a high five in the hall, as he proudly informed me he secured a donation from the Carmichaels. He was killing the donation-game for the Angel Program, which actually kind of made me get more into the fundraiser, as well. I even went to The Bean last night to check on the Angel Tree and pawned off some snowflakes on unsuspecting customers. It seemed we had formed some sort of truce, and it wasn't lost on me that it only took us nine years to do so. But whatever. *Progress is progress, right?*

I crammed my books into my locker and grabbed my book bag. Friday night signified Netflix and pizza with Ethan. It also meant a solid evening away from home, which would be short-lived excitement because this particular Friday also happened to be the start of winter break. Two whole weeks off before we returned to school, two whole weeks at home.

I took my time gathering my things since I was waiting for Ethan anyway, when two long arms pinned me to my locker, resting on either side of me. Arms too muscled to be Ethan's.

My heart leapt in my throat as I caught the scent of his cologne. It smelled of cedarwood and spice. And I knew from my recent time spent with him, it was Carson.

The thought of his warm body pressing into mine sent my pulse into fits. Swallowing, I turned around, pushing myself as far into my locker as possible because he was mind-numbingly close in proximity.

"Hey, Shorty." Though he dropped his arms, he stayed right where he was, invading my personal space.

I narrowed my eyes at the nickname, but the glare didn't hold. "Did you want to talk about the Angel Tree? I think we'll be set to collect the presents and remaining tags then go shopping soon since there's only a week left."

"Yeah, sure. I mean, that's not what I came to talk to you about, but that sounds good."

"Oh. Well, what's up?" *Why was I so nervous?*

"I'm sure you heard about my party on Saturday."

"Yeah," I drawled. The conversation with Lauren on Monday felt like forever ago.

"I think you should come."

"You do?" I stared up at him in disbelief. "You're inviting me?"

"You were never not invited," he said, rolling his eyes. "But, yes, this is me officially inviting you."

"Um, why?"

Carson laughed and reached out, tucking a lock of hair behind my ear, sending shock waves up my spine. "Don't overthink this, Mia. It will be fun."

"Fun," I repeated stupidly.

Why couldn't I just not talk?

"Yeah, fun. I believe Merriam-Webster describes it as something that provides amusement or enjoyment."

"Ha-ha, I know what fun is."

He grinned. "You might have to prove it." He winked and took a couple steps back, further into the hallway. "So, I'll see you there." He pointed at me. "Eight o'clock tomorrow night."

I reached out as if to bring him back. "But I didn't—"

"Don't overthink it," he said again, then turned and hurried away before I could say no.

I dropped my arms by my side, then turned back to my locker and screamed inside to muffle the sound. When I emerged, Ethan leaned against the locker next to mine, brow raised. "What was that?"

"Huh? Nothing. Just your brother. . ." And an epic freak-out on my part. Carry on.

"Yep, I got that part. It was definitely Carson, but it also looked like you and Carson flirting."

I rolled my eyes. "We were not flirting."

"Well, I don't know what *you* were doing, exactly. You looked more like a deer in headlights, but that was definitely Carson flirting."

"It was not," I said, but my voice cracked, betraying me. Was he flirting? Now that I thought about it, his behavior was a little suspect. And why did that give me butterflies?

Ethan's smile faded. He stepped close, hastily shoving my hair from my face and said in a breathy whisper, "Don't overthink it, Mia." Then he stepped back and guffawed. "You should've seen your face!" He pointed, laughing harder.

I smacked him. "You're hilarious." Glaring, I asked, "Are you ready to go or what?"

"Yeah," he said through the tears forming in his eyes. "Let's go."

Once we were in my car, headed away from the school and toward the coast, Ethan turned to me. "So, are you going to actually go?"

I glanced over at him warily. Ethan and I had never attended one of Carson's parties, which might sound weird, but when you factored in how Carson and I couldn't stand each other, it made perfect sense.

But something was changing. And I did want to go. Not *for* Carson, of course. Call it curiosity. Boredom. Call it. . . I shrugged. "I don't know. I wouldn't mind seeing what all the hype is about."

Ethan grunted in response, and I realized he was going to make me work for it. He was my best friend. He knew what I thought before I did. His silence told me he was going to make me ask. "I'll only go if you go. Will you please, please go with me?"

"Are you sure Carson wants his little brother hanging around? It might put a damper on things."

I rolled my eyes as I took the turn onto my street. "Be serious."

Ethan grinned and his hazel eyes danced

with laughter. "What? I am. I saw the way he was looking at you. I'd have to be blind not to. If there's one thing I'm sure of, it's that Carson wants you at his party, and he wants you alone." Ethan made an obnoxious kissing face, complete with sound effects.

I reached over and punched him in the arm. "Ew. Shut up."

Ethan laughed. "Just don't say I didn't warn ya."

CHAPTER EIGHT

I entered the Brooks' home like I was entering a war zone—slowly and carefully as if at any moment, I might hit a landmine hidden underneath the gleaming hardwood. Enough time had passed since Carson invited me that I had myself half convinced this was some sort of trap. It didn't matter that Ethan was by my side or that we just came from Luigi's where we shared a large pepperoni (of which Ethan ate eighty percent his weight in pizza dough and cheese). Nothing could ease the giant knot fisting in the center of my stomach.

Ethan groaned. "I can't believe you talked me into coming to one of Carson's parties. This is so lame."

I ignored him as I bolstered my own courage

and led the way through the foyer into the living room. Music played in the background, and about twelve other seniors mingled about, talking, and sipping from red plastic cups. I waved to a couple people, then turned back to Ethan. "It doesn't look so bad."

He shot me a skeptical look. "Tell me that when you're dared to go streaking through the neighborhood later."

A surge of panic coursed through my veins. "Wait, they don't actually do things like that, right?" I asked, but Ethan ignored me.

Despite being well-liked, it had been a while since I attended a party, so it felt a bit like shaking the rust off.

"Does he have anything to drink in here or what?" Ethan asked.

He made a beeline for the kitchen, and I hurried after him, only a little frightened at the image he put in my head. "No one would dare me to do that," I said, unable to let it go. I still had this horrifying vision of being forced to streak in front of the class, and worse of all, in front of Carson.

"Really?" Ethan raised a brow. "You don't think your arch nemesis would dare you to do something humiliating?"

I swallowed. It was like Ethan was inside my brain, verbalizing my fears. "Carson and I have been getting along lately." *Sorta.* "Weren't you just teasing me about it yesterday at school?"

He shrugged, which only annoyed me more.

I grumbled and crossed my arms over my chest as Ethan helped himself to a beer and shoved a plastic cup of something fruity in my hand. When I gave it a sniff, my mouth watered. It smelled like strawberries and oranges. I took a healthy gulp and nearly barfed. "Ugh. This stuff is horrendous. What's in here, cough syrup?"

"I've been told it's Carson's secret concoction. It loosens you up."

"Wait. Loosen me up for what—"

"You came." Carson appeared in the entryway to the kitchen, seemingly out of nowhere.

I snapped my mouth shut, my throat suddenly dry as I took in his somewhat rumpled appearance. He wore dark jeans and a long sleeve button-down shirt, which was untucked, rolled at the sleeves, and open at the neck to reveal a small triangle of tanned skin.

"You brought lil bro," he said, eyeing Ethan as he drew closer. "You're late. I thought maybe you'd chickened out."

"Why would I chicken out?" I croaked. Then, calmer, I added, "We were just hanging out, catching dinner, and lost track of time." I motioned to Ethan.

It was a lie. Our tardiness was entirely orchestrated because I hadn't wanted to be one of the first ones there.

He nodded as if he understood, and when Ethan sidled up beside me, his gaze zoned in on us, scrutinizing as he glanced back and forth. "Right.

Well, have fun," he said, clinking his cup to mine. "Party games start in five." Then he left, heading back into the living room.

"Wow. That was pretty civil," Ethan said. "Maybe you guys have finally called a truce. See? Trying to strangle him worked to your advantage."

I gave him a sidelong look, and he laughed, but I couldn't help a little twinge of disappointment that Carson hadn't stayed to chat longer.

"Hey, Ethan, what's up, man?" Drake Brown, another junior, came up beside him, then offered him a fist-bump.

I sighed inwardly. Great. Drake was on the football team with Ethan, which meant if they stood there for any length of time, they'd start talking football and never stop.

"I'm glad I'm not the only junior here," Drake added, then glanced down at me, needling me in the ribs. "I'm surprised to see you here though, after the basketball incident and everything," he said, gesturing toward my eye.

"Right." I nodded. Even the junior boys knew about it. "Well, Carson and I have to work on the Angel Program together, so we've kind of been forced to get along. He probably invited me to be nice."

"Okay," Drake drawled like he didn't believe it.

"Seriously," I said because the more I said it, the more authentic it felt. Carson was simply being cordial.

"Yeah. I believe you." He shot Ethan a look that said he didn't believe it at all.

But I wasn't about to let it go.

"What? What was that look?" I said, pointing between them.

Drake shifted on his feet then ran a hand through his bleach blonde locks. "It's just. . . Carson's kind of a pot-stirrer. He likes shaking things up, giving people something to talk about. You two usually don't get along. I'm just saying that if he invited you, he probably had a reason."

My throat instantly dried. It hurt to swallow.

What if Carson did invite me there in some epic plan to embarrass me?

I glanced toward the living room, my gaze latching onto Carson, who was chatting up Olivia. I hadn't even seen her come in.

Lauren's words from Monday came back to me. *I heard Olivia's on the prowl, and she plans on crashing.*

Great.

I groaned inwardly, trying to ease the nerves jumping in my belly. He barely said two words to me when I came in, but there he was, bent forward at the waist, so Olivia could whisper something in his ear. He frowned as he listened, then suddenly, his eyes lifted to mine, and my stomach dropped.

I snapped my head back toward Ethan and Drake, cheeks flushed. Maybe this hadn't been such a great idea, after all. I had the terrible urge to leave. Coming suddenly seemed like a horrible idea. What had I been thinking? Now that Carson and I were working on a project together, we could somehow be friends and get along? And why did I even want to?

I turned and focused back on Ethan's conversation with Drake, I tried to follow along, but they were using football-speak, and I was lost.

I sipped my drink—probably a little quicker than I should've—but it dulled the edge of my nerves, and before I knew it, the party didn't seem so bad. The slightly fuzzy feeling in my head had me more relaxed than I'd been in weeks, maybe months. Until Carson's voice rose above the music.

"Truth or dare," he yelled. "Starts in two. Let's go."

"I think that's our calling," Drake said. "We'd better get in there. Mandy Peters is here, and I'm hoping to ask her to the Snowflake Ball. I've been dragging my feet and I'm, like, the last person I know to get a date."

"Not the last," Ethan muttered under his breath, which earned him a jab to the ribs.

He laughed and said bye to Drake, as I muttered, "Thanks a lot, *bud*."

Ethan chuckled and grabbed me, pulling me in a headlock. "Don't worry, you're going to that dance," he promised.

"So you say."

As he dragged me toward the living room, I asked, "Do we have to do this?"

Ethan gave me a look that said I was a wimp. "Come on. Are you really going to let him scare you off over a little game of truth or dare?"

"If it means keeping my clothes on, then, yes," I said eyeing everyone around me.

Ethan snorted. "You'll be fine. You only go if someone picks you. Just choose truth," he said with a shrug.

I groaned and begrudgingly followed Ethan and took a seat on the floor in front of the sofa. Everyone but a couple kids, several of which were making out in the corner, took a seat.

Carson turned and adjusted the volume of the music on the surround sound unit. I remembered the day they got it. When we were thirteen, Mr. Brooks came home with a giant television and the stereo system. By the time he figured out how to install it, the sky outside turned to dusk, but Ethan and I waited patiently, then stayed up late watching Jaws with the sound blasting. The next day, we went to the beach and were so paranoid about a shark being in the surf, we kept running onto shore. Carson called us babies.

Everyone gathered around the room in a circle, taking their places. Olivia sat several seats away from Carson, giggling and flipping her blonde locks over her shoulder in the most obnoxious way. Only when Maddie took the spot on my right, did I sigh in relief. A lot of guys liked her.

Surely, she was more interesting than I was. With her next to me, I'd probably be left alone. Or at least I hoped.

Ethan squeezed my arm as Carson briefly went over the rules, which, of course, everyone already knew. When he finished, he glanced to Ethan and added, "Also, let's keep it semi-clean, folks. My baby brother's here tonight." He winked at Ethan before turning his gaze away.

"Idiot," Ethan muttered like it didn't even faze him, but I could feel him tense slightly beside me, and when I turned my gaze back to Carson, he was watching me, gauging my reaction.

"Mia, you start," Carson announced.

"What? Me?" I pointed to myself. "But I—"

"You gotta pay to play. Come on," Carson said, grinning.

I wanted to punch him in the nose he looked so smug. Of course he wasn't going to let me blend into the background. That would be *nice*. This was his way of reminding everyone I was there.

"Fine." I clutched my cup out in front of me and shot Maddie a look of apology as I said, "Maddie, truth or dare."

She didn't seem to mind as she bit her lip and debated, then said, "Truth."

"Okay. . ." I hedged, mostly because I couldn't think of anything. After a long silence, I went with the only thing I could think of. "Is it true you and Pete Wolfe went skinny dipping at his going away party during the summer?"

Maddie laughed, eyes sparkling. She looked confident as she said, "Well, I had to give him something to remember me by, didn't I?"

Alrighty, then...

Maddie took a sip of her drink as she scanned the room, looking for her next victim, while I had the luxury of relaxing since the rules stated she couldn't turn around and choose me.

When her gaze landed on Ethan beside me, I wondered if he was nervous, but he looked fine. "Ethan, truth or dare." A grin snaked over her girlish features, and suddenly, I had a bad feeling about this.

With confidence, he said, "Truth."

Maddie merely grinned wider. She didn't seem displeased in his selection. "Have you ever liked Mia as something more than friends?"

I snorted. *Nice try.*

I glanced to Ethan, shooting him a look. The question was so ridiculous, it was laughable. Ethan and I had never been anything more than the best of friends.

Beside me, Ethan cursed. "Yes."

I froze, and my heart banged against my ribs.

I misheard. It was the only explanation.

Slowly, I shook my head as if to clear my hearing, then turned to him, sure I had gotten it wrong. Ethan was the peanut butter to my jelly. We just worked well together, were always on the same page. But we were never anything more than friends. Not even close.

I heard someone snicker and mutter, "Oh, snap." And then the room grew utterly silent. Probably because I stared at the side of Ethan's face— now fire-engine red—for what felt like a millennium, waiting for the "gotcha moment" where he laughed and said he fooled me.

Finally, he turned to face me and rolled his eyes as he leaned in, so no one else could hear, and whispered, "Relax, Mia. It was when I was like ten or eleven and for like two months."

When he straightened, I squinted at him, like my narrowed lids could detect lies. He was telling the truth. I knew this because Ethan had a tick. When he lied, he blinked and scratched his nose.

I nodded as if this made perfect sense, although it was still news to me, and I wasn't sure how I felt about it. Ethan and I never kept secrets from each other, much less one like *that*.

"Okay, my turn," Ethan said, and he pursed his lips, his expression serious, which I found weird because he had acted as though this whole party was lame and now all of a sudden, he was into it?

His gaze locked on Olivia with a devious glint in his eye. I knew he couldn't stand her, so this would be interesting. "Olivia, truth or dare."

She looked him dead in the eye, and said, "Dare, of course," like we were wimps for choosing truth.

"Kiss my brother."

My jaw dropped. Even a flicker of surprise ran through Olivia's eyes before she turned her cat-like gaze on Carson with a grin. I watched Carson's response. It was no surprise he seemed unfazed. He merely smirked and sauntered across the room. Leaning down, he gave Olivia a chaste kiss on the lips, then pulled away.

Everyone around him protested, and like the conductor of an orchestra, Ethan waved his arms beside me, slashing through the air and everyone hushed. "I don't think so. A real kiss. Kiss her like you mean it. Isn't that what you supposedly said to Wes and Lauren a few months ago?"

Everyone around him laughed, which didn't bode well for Carson's ego. I wondered how he was handling all of this. He was so unused to being the one goaded. Unless it was by me.

Carson drilled a murderous look at Ethan. The little muscle above his jaw flickered. And I had the most thrilling, yet confusing thought. He doesn't want to kiss her.

A guy not wanting to kiss Olivia Matthews was practically unheard of.

His gaze shifted, landing on me for a moment, so quick I barely registered it before he turned back to Olivia.

Smiling, he knelt down in front of her and placed a finger under her chin. My stomach roiled as he said, "Let's do this." Then his lips were on hers, kissing her, slow and soft before Olivia, like the vampire she was, gripped the front of his shirt and pulled him in even closer.

They were like a pack of wolves then, kissing ferociously—like they needed each other to breathe, to live. One feeding off of the other.

It made me sick to my stomach

Everyone catcalled around them. Some whistled. A boy in the back, said, "Way to go Brooks."

I couldn't tell you how the kiss ended. Looking away was about the only thing I could do to keep the fruity drink I consumed from making a reappearance. When they finally pulled away, Carson smiled a lazy, victorious smile and returned to his seat. Only a second later, his eyes found mine, and he winked.

My cheeks caught fire, and I glanced away, hating myself for it. I should've held his gaze. Now I probably just looked like a boring prude. Like I couldn't even handle a little lip-lock without blushing. Or worse yet, like him kissing her bothered me.

Little did he know I was merely trying to suppress my gag reflex at the thought of anyone having to swap spit with him.

When Olivia finally wiped the delirious look from her face, she said, "Carson, truth or dare?"

Carson hesitated, then said, "Truth."

The look on Olivia's face told me she was disappointed, but then she brightened, and asked,

"Out of everyone in this room, who would you want to kiss the most?" She smiled like the Cheshire Cat, clearly thinking he'd name her following their little tongue war.

I rolled my eyes. No doubt she'd get what she wanted, and they'd go have some epic battle of tonsil hockey in the back of the room.

Carson rubbed the back of his neck with his hand, as if contemplating something, then said, "Shorty."

My gaze snapped to his. *What?*

"Who?" Olivia said.

"Randalls." He shrugged like it was nothing. Like he didn't just tell the entire room that he wanted to kiss his enemy. "I'd kiss Randalls."

Olivia glanced to me with bloodlust in her eyes. For a moment, I thought I might need a cross and a couple bulbs of garlic to ward her off.

I could hear the surrounding whispers, and I could imagine what everyone was saying. *Me and Carson? No way. It was cataclysmic. Apocalyptic.*

Across the room, Jeremiah Dermot crowed, "Oh, now we all know why you made Brad Sousa dump her, and there's all this tension between you too. Why don't you guys just kiss it out, huh?"

My pulse drummed in my ears, and I had no doubt my face was redder than a tomato. I frowned, ignoring Jeremiah's prattling because it made zero sense. Brad Sousa? He broke up with me freshman year.

My gaze shifted back to Carson again, and he

broke out into one of his trademark, cocky grins. And I knew. He was merely trying to mess with my head. Of course this was all one big joke to him. For a moment, I actually believed him.

How foolish.

Tell Mia you want to kiss her and watch her ensuing panic.

I narrowed my eyes on him, furious with myself for thinking for even a moment he might actually be serious. Then someone to the right of me shouted, "Prove it."

I swallowed, flicking my gaze toward the voice. But it was no longer one voice. Everyone started chanting, "Prove it! Prove it! Prove it!" Like this was a game and we were in a football stadium.

It was my worst nightmare come true. Worse than the dream where I stood in front of the whole class in my underwear. Worse than having to go streaking through the Brooks' living room on a dare.

Carson's plan was probably to kiss me just so he could spin some kind of lie about how awful a kisser I was. My reputation would never recover.

Well, I've got news for you, buddy, I might not have gobs of experience, but I'm a dang good kisser.

But his lips weren't even worthy of touching mine, which is why I glanced to Ethan and let my expression do the talking. My eyes pleaded with him.

Ethan's mouth was set in a half-grimace,

half smile. "Guys, it's not a dare, remember?" Ethan said. "It's not happening."

At that moment, I had never been more grateful. Ethan earned every bit of the label of my best friend.

"Ethan's right. And this is my mouth. I'll kiss who I want," I said, staring Carson dead in the eyes in challenge.

There were a few boos from the peanut gallery before Carson grumbled at them to shut up and started, "Ethan, truth or dare?"

"Seriously, dude?"

Carson merely raised a brow at Ethan's less than enthused response.

"Truth."

I sensed Ethan didn't want to risk playing kissing-buddies with anyone, hence his choice.

"Have you ever kissed Mia?" Carson asked.

I frowned. Clearly, this was a reaction from the question earlier, but why? Why did Carson care?

"No," Ethan answered, his voice hard.

Relief flickered through Carson's eyes as he sat back, looking satisfied.

Then, Ethan turned to me, and I wondered why he was looking at me like that before he murmured, "I have to see something. Just trust me."

My stomach tumbled, still processing his words because I sensed a weird kind of war brewing. One I wasn't privy too. Like someone had a secret they weren't telling me and here I was just stumbling in the dark.

"Mia, truth or dare?" Ethan asked.

It was a good thing we were already on the ground because I would've fallen off my chair. Why on earth was he asking me? He knew I didn't even want to play this stupid game. In my head, I took back every nice, loving thing I had ever felt about him. Best friend? *Pfft.*

All the questions already asked drifted through my head. So far, Ethan had confessed to having a crush on me when he was eleven. Carson admitted he wanted to kiss me. Maddie had announced she skinny dipped. What deep-seated secrets of mine would be revealed?

I was probably one of the most boring girls on the planet, but I had no doubt if there was something embarrassing to be unearthed, it would be drudged up during a brutal high school game of truth or dare.

And though Ethan was my best friend, the way he was looking at me—with a poker face I had never seen before—for the first time since we became friends, I wasn't sure I could trust him with my secrets. I don't think I would've trusted anyone at that moment, so I said, "Dare." Because there was no way my best friend would make me go streaking.

"Kiss me," he said.

"What?" I blinked at him, sure I misheard.

Everyone around me froze. You could hear a pin drop.

"You heard me. Kiss me," Ethan said, and though his playful expression was back—my Ethan, my best friend—his words were all wrong.

As I tried to process them, I glanced around at the familiar faces surrounding us.

"Um. . ." I hedged, weighing my options. I could run out of the room like a baby and solidify myself as a loser for the remainder of the year, or I could just do it.

But this was Ethan, my best friend in the whole wide world. He may as well be my brother. Why did he even ask me to do this? There was clearly something going on I was unaware of.

"This is stupid," Carson said.

My head snapped toward him. Of all the people to come to my rescue, I did not expect it to be him.

"Is it?" Ethan asked. "Because isn't this how you play? Mia picked dare, so I dared her to kiss me. What's the problem? Unless, of course, you don't want me to."

Next to me, Maddie rested her chin in her hand, eyes bright, grinning like she was watching a new episode of Stranger Things, while Drake snickered.

Carson's mouth flattened into a thin line before he opened his mouth and said, "Why would I care—"

"I don't feel well," I said, jumping up. "I'm done. You guys finish without me."

It wasn't the most graceful exit as I stumbled over people's feet, unable to get out of the room fast enough. Behind me, they booed and moaned. I think I even heard someone call me a cry baby, which was really just great. First, I'm labeled a psycho after my incident with Carson in gym class, and now everyone will think I'm a total wimp.

"You know what? I don't even care," I mumbled to myself as I stepped inside the kitchen, pacing like a caged tiger.

I rounded the island and leaned back on it, glad to be alone for a minute. Even though I tried to make sense of what just happened, I couldn't. My head pounded from the effort, or maybe it was the alcohol. First, Ethan admitted he had a crush on me, even though he claimed it was when we were little. Then, Carson said he wanted to kiss me after his epic lip lock with Olivia. Though I'm pretty sure that was all a part of his master plan to annihilate me once and for all, and then Ethan asked *me* to kiss *him*. What. The. Heck.

This evening almost made me wish I had stayed home. But after being grounded, other than to work on the Angel Program for the last two weeks, I was finally free, and the last thing I wanted to do was go back to my house when both of my parents would be home. As awful as this party was, I had no desire to play witness to the ensuing conflict of WWIII.

I was deliberating hiding in the bathroom as an alternative when someone entered the kitchen. I shoved my shoulders back and spun around, expecting Ethan.

But it wasn't Ethan. It was Carson.

He stood in the entryway, hands in his pockets, head bowed.

Well, at least he had the decency to look sheepish.

I squared my shoulders and tipped my chin, ready for a fight. When he stepped closer, I couldn't help myself as I asked, "Why'd you invite me here? Was it just to embarrass me? Because if that's the case, then congratulations. You win."

Carson exhaled and raked a hand through his thick brown hair. "I invited you because I wanted you here."

"But why?"

"I wanted to see you. Outside of school. Outside of the Angel Tree stuff. But I didn't think you'd bring Ethan. I mean, I guess I should've known. You guys do everything together, but. . ." He shrugged.

"What was that out there?" I asked, motioning toward the living room. It sounded like the others had continued without us, and I briefly wondered if Ethan was still playing along.

Carson rounded the island until he stood beside me. "I'm not sure I know what you mean."

My hands fisted by my side until my fingernails dug into my palms. "You don't know what I mean? Okay, how about when Olivia asked you, out of anyone in the room, who you'd kiss, and you said my name. What about that, huh? Was that just to make me feel stupid? So you could kiss me then make fun of me after? And what about the thing Jeremiah said about Brad Sousa? Then there was Ethan. All those questions and then you acted all —"

"Slow down." Carson shifted to face me and placed a hand on each of my biceps. "Breathe," he coaxed, and the corners of his mouth pulled up into a smile. "That was a lot of questions.

It was a lot of things to confuse me, I wanted to say, but instead, I remained silent, trying to ignore the heat of his palms burning into my skin.

"The thing Jer said?"

I nodded.

"You dated Brad Sousa your freshman year."

Losing my patience, I scowled and said, "I know when I dated him. He asked me out, and we went on one date before he dumped me. He claimed it was him, not me, which everyone knows is code for *it really is you; I just don't want to hurt your feelings*."

Carson laughed. "Or it was because I told him that you were secretly into girls and that you were just using him as a front so your parents didn't find out."

I gasped as the horror of what he just told me sunk in. "No," I drawled.

He pursed his lips. "Guilty."

I allowed that to sink in a moment. *So that's why he was always giving me and Kira funny looks during science lab.* "That is wrong on so many levels," I said.

Carson's cheeks flushed in a way that I was pretty sure was an indicator of guilt. As I stared up at him, my entire high school love life started flashing in my head. Guys would seem so into me, and then—boom—out of nowhere they'd turn cold, and it was as if I never stood a chance.

I opened my mouth, then closed it again, my question stuck in the back of my throat. Carson wasn't that cruel, was he?

Who was I kidding?

"When Pete Wolfe asked me to homecoming—"

"I told him you kiss like a dog."

My eyes widened as anger welled up inside me like a geyser, ready to blow. "Last year, Robby Mason told everyone he was asking me to junior prom. Then at the last minute, he changed his mind and asked someone else, and I had to go with Ethan."

Carson pulled a face; one I couldn't decipher. There was something he wasn't telling me.

I pointed at him. "What? What is that face?" I poked him in the ribs, and his hands tightened around my arms.

"He might've decided not to ask you because he heard your dad showed up on a date once with a loaded shotgun."

"What? That's not true. My dad doesn't even

own a—"

Laughter ripped from his chest.

Glaring, I said, "*You* told him that?"

"I may or may not have let it slip at one of my parties."

"But why?"

He shrugged. "I didn't want you to go with him."

"Because...?"

"Which one? Robby? He has chronic halitosis. Trust me, I did you a favor."

My hands fisted at my side as a wave of anger shot through me. How dare he take my choices away. I could've given him some mints, gum, something! "Let me get this straight," I said through gritted teeth. "You're trying to claim that you saved me from bad breath?"

"You're welcome." His blue eyes sparkled. I wanted to cover them with my hands because they were too beautiful for someone so rude.

"How many times have you done this? Scared boys away?"

"I don't know. Only a few times."

I stepped forward, pushing him back until he was up against the counter. "Why? Do you really hate me that much?" I asked, mortified at the way my voice cracked. Any second I'd burst into tears, and then I'd really look like an idiot.

"I don't hate you, Mia," he murmured.

I tried to shove him again, but he had nowhere to go, so instead, he pulled me closer. And as he slid his hands up and down my arms, I shivered. Even when he tipped my chin up to meet his eyes, goosebumps covered my skin everywhere he touched.

What was he doing?

Then he leaned down and whispered in the shell of my ear, "I'm sorry." When he pulled away, his gaze was soft on mine.

My breath caught in my throat, burning in my lungs—an inferno inside my chest. The flames ate me alive as his gaze flickered to my mouth.

On an inhale, I mustered my courage because I needed to know. Right now, he wasn't acting like he hated me. Not at all. He was looking at me like maybe he liked me, like he wanted to kiss me. And the craziest thing was that I kind of wanted him to.

I swallowed. "Back there, when you said you wanted to kiss me. . ."

"Yeah?" he asked.

"Did you mean it?"

His eyes zeroed in on my mouth. When he leaned down, his lips hovering above mine,

I squeezed my eyes closed. Every nerve ending stood at attention. My breathing rasped in and out of my lungs, while my pulse pounded in my ears. Everything around me was magnified times one thousand.

"What do you think?" he whispered.

CHAPTER NINE

"Carson!" Jeremiah Dermot yelled from the hallway.

My eyes fluttered open, and I was staring straight into the dazzling blue of Carson's eyes. His hand slid to the back of my neck, pulling me closer. I could practically feel his lips on mine before Jeremiah yelled again. "Dude, let's go, man!"

Carson sighed, then straightened just as Jeremiah and Greg ambled into the kitchen. "Yo man, you're supposed to be our DD and drive us home. And we need to jet."

Grumbling, Carson squeezed his eyes closed, and said, "Okay. Just one second. Be right there."

Then he turned back to me. "Crap. I totally forgot they had to leave early, and I promised them..."

"It's fine," I said, feeling equal parts relieved and desperate for him to stay.

"Be here when I get back?" His eyes scanned my face earnestly, causing my stomach to turn inside out.

"Yeah, sure," I said.

He nodded and flashed me a megawatt smile before he turned to the guys. "Okay, pin-heads, let's go."

Once he was gone, I exhaled and spun around toward the counter. Leaning forward, I pressed my forehead into a kitchen cabinet. After my interaction with Carson and our almost-kiss, I wasn't sure I could stand upright without the added support.

What the heck just happened? I almost locked lips with Carson Brooks. My insides squeezed at the thought.

"You know he doesn't really like you, right?" Olivia called from behind me.

My head snapped up, and I spun around to face her in all her snotty bleach-blonde glory. Her overly lipsticked mouth spread into a smile as she drew closer. "He only invited you because he feels sorry for you."

I swallowed. "How do you know that?"

"He told me." Olivia glanced down to her manicure like she was talking about the weather and not crushing my spirit. After a moment, she turned her eyes back to mine and added, "I just thought you should know. I mean, as your friend and all. I'd hate for you to get hurt."

"Right," I said, though I had no illusions as to how much of a friend to me Olivia really was. "Um, thanks."

"No problem." She shrugged. "Us girls gotta stick together."

Just as she spun around to leave the kitchen, Ethan appeared in the entryway. Sidestepping him like the plague, she disappeared into the living room.

Hand in pockets and looking sheepish, Ethan strolled toward me. "What did she want?"

I shrugged. "Oh, you know, the usual." I stared at Ethan, my emotions a tangle of knots with the knowledge that he disappointed me tonight. Suddenly, I was tired. Spent. I didn't know whether to believe Olivia or not, but I wasn't sure it even mattered. Carson Brooks and I hooking up was the craziest thing I could think of.

"Hey, about the game in there. . ." Ethan drew closer and reached out to nudge me in the arm. "I'm sorry. I acted like an idiot. I just wanted to test a theory."

"A theory?" I asked, hating the way my throat ached. Why did I feel like I was going to cry?

"I wanted to see if Carson likes you."

"Oh." I swallowed. "And your conclusion?"

His hazel eyes crinkled at the corners with his half-smile. "Inconclusive. I can't tell if this is just another one of his games or if he really is into you."

"Well, no worries because I'm pretty sure I know the answer."

Ethan said nothing to that. Instead, he paused and glanced around. "Where is he anyway?"

"He left to give Greg and Jeremiah a ride home. They were too drunk to drive, and I guess he had promised."

Ethan nodded. "Wanna leave and go hang out?"

I sighed and glanced around the kitchen. I didn't want to be there when Carson got back. Whatever happened between us was over, and Olivia's words had hit their mark. I didn't know whether to trust my gut—that feeling I had when Carson was drawing me close, his lips about to crush mine—or my head which told me we never stood a chance. We hated each other. That's the way it's always been. Our rivalry was inevitable.

No use changing that.

"Um, no. I think I'm just going to call it a night. You'd better stay, though. I know Carson will only be a few minutes, but one of you should be here at your house."

"You're leaving?" Ethan asked.

I knew what he was thinking—I must be desperate to get out of there if it meant returning home. And he'd be right.

"Yeah. I think so." I stepped forward and pulled Ethan into a hug, then headed for the door.

#

It was the start of winter break. For most kids my age, that marked the start of freedom, of staying up late and sleeping in. It meant Christmas movies, cozying up with hot chocolate, a plate of cookies, and shopping, some of my favorite things. But lately, my favorite things no longer seemed to matter. At least not like they used to. There was no holiday spirit at home. The typical joy of Christmas had dulled. I no longer looked forward to weekends, let alone two weeks off school, because it meant spending more time at home. Sure, I'd spend as much of it with Ethan as I could, and I'd hang with some of my other friends, but they had their own families, their own holiday festivities to attend to, most of which wouldn't include me. Ultimately, nothing changed my reality—that this Christmas wouldn't be merry or jolly or bright.

I sat in my room; earbuds crammed into my ears as far as possible, though I hadn't needed them (yet). I gave my parents a couple hours before they found something worth fighting over.

Usually, I'd call Ethan, but considering my less than stellar mood, I decided to wait until I was out of my funk. Why drag him down with me? Plus, I still felt awkward about the party, everything too fresh to ignore.

I flipped the pages of my pocket calendar to today's date. Everyone else my age preferred using their phone for everything, but I preferred a paper calendar. There was something oddly satisfying about being able to write things down, then physically scratch items off a to-do list.

Until now.

Now I hated the little blank squares and numbers marking time because for every box I drew an X through, I grew closer to the deadline for receiving an early acceptance. Pretty soon, I will have run out of time, and I was pretty much guaranteed a rejection letter.

I gripped my pen tightly and put an X through today's date. The mail had already come. There was nothing for me. Sighing, I flopped back in my bed, and an earbud popped loose.

It was Monday, and Carson and I should be

working on the Angel Program. We needed to do the remaining shopping for the kid's gifts and the leftover tags on the Angel Tree, but my motivation was severely lacking. I wasn't sure how to face him after the party on Saturday night. Olivia's words continued to run through my head, and the more they did, the more accurate they seemed. After all, I was there. I saw the way he kissed her. That was not the kiss of a boy who liked someone else.

I covered my face and moaned. Why was I even thinking about Carson? He was nothing to me. I needed to forget that whole awful party. The way Ethan and Carson embarrassed me. The way Carson looked at me with those soulful eyes, like he wanted to kiss me.

I rolled onto my side and closed my eyes. The sound of my parent's voices carried up the stairs, to the ear where the bud had come loose. Typically, I blocked them out, but at the moment, I was feeling oddly masochistic and reveling in my truth, so I plucked the earbuds out entirely by the chord and listened to the disjointed sound of their voices.

"I just want to know. . .worth it. . ." my mother said.

"Maybe if you were actually. . .when you're here. . ."

"That's ridiculous."

"...call it like I see it..."

"Whatever," my mother's anger radiated from the floor below.

The doorbell rang, and I tensed, wondering which neighbor had heard them fighting this time. The other night, Mrs. Wheeler had come knocking on the door to make sure everything was all right.

Nope. It's okay, Mrs. Wheeler, you know, just another one of the Randall's blowouts, I wanted to say. Instead, with shame burning in my gut, I told her I'd ask them to keep it down.

I listened, waiting for my parents to answer the door, but they didn't even pause in their fighting this time. Even when the doorbell competed to be heard, their voices rose.

Shooting up from my bed, I hurried across my room and peered out the window facing the road. My eyes focused on the old, black Jeep Wrangler sitting in our driveway, and my stomach turned in on itself. It was Carson's Jeep.

I didn't walk down the stairs, I ran. My feet pounded over the creaking stair treads, each thump of my foot bringing me closer to the door, while my insides screamed, *Don't let him hear. Please, don't let him hear.*

My feet hit the landing, and off to my right, I caught sight of my parents, standing toe-to-toe. Mom pointed in Dad's face. Tears streamed down her cheeks as her voice reached epic proportions. Nails on a chalkboard had nothing on her other-worldly screeching.

In a rush, I flung the door open and stepped outside, slamming it closed behind me. My chest rose and fell in a rapid staccato as I tried to calm my breathing and gain control, but it was no use. I realized much too late that I was standing only inches from Carson. I peered up into his eyes, the color so vibrant it was nearly alive and churning like the ocean. The scent of his cologne wafted toward me, and I had to fight the urge to lean into him. To inhale all that cedarwood and spice and let it comfort me.

"Uh, now's not really a good time," I said weakly. My cheeks heated with embarrassment as my parent's screaming match carried through the door. There wasn't steel thick enough to block out the sound of them. As if my first encounter with him after his party weren't tense enough.

"I thought we'd go shopping for the Angel Program. We have less than a week now."

"Right. True. But we could go tomorrow. I'll meet you at your house," I said, placing my hands on his shoulders and spinning him around.

Carson easily shrugged me off and turned back toward me, his mouth turned down into a frown. "No." Carson shook his head.

"No?" I stared at him, incredulous.

"No. We're going now. Come on. Swim practice is over, and I have no plans but to spend the rest of the day shopping with you. Let's go."

I glanced back to the closed door. "But. . .I don't have my things."

"You don't need anything."

I bit my lip. "My purse, and my wallet. . ."

From inside the house, my father's voice boomed, "I'm so sick of this," he shouted, and I jumped.

Training my gaze on the ground, I was unable to meet Carson's eyes. The only thing worse than facing your nemesis after an awkward evening was facing him when your world was falling apart. It put you on uneven footing.

But Carson never went easy on me. It wasn't his style. Instead, he pressed his fingers under my chin, tilting my gaze up to his, making me face him. "Come on. I'll buy us dinner afterward," he coaxed. "All you need are shoes and a jacket," he said, glancing down to my socked feet.

When I didn't budge, he added, "Please."

And there it was. That same look he had Saturday night in his kitchen, the one that told me he wanted to kiss me. The one that told me maybe he and I could be more than enemies.

I shoved down the ache in the back of my throat and signaled for him to wait as I ran inside, retrieving a pair of boots and a jacket from the coat closet in the hallway as quickly as possible. I didn't even bother to tell my parents I was going out because the chances of them even noticing were slim to none. These days, when I wasn't at school or with Ethan, I spent nearly all my time cooped up in my room.

Once I popped back outside, I hurried down the sidewalk where Carson waited for me by his Jeep. My heart swelled then. Carson had given me a Get Out of Jail Free card, and I intended to use it.

CHAPTER TEN

I settled into Carson's Jeep and surveyed my sur-roundings. It was my first time being in his car, and like his room, it smelled of him—a combination of chlorine from the pool and cologne. Nothing was out of place, and it appeared that he took excellent care of it.

After I buckled my seatbelt, he started the engine and twisted in his seat so he could back down my driveway. Avoiding my eye, he said, "Mia, about the other night..."

I shook my head. "Forget it," I said. Because I wanted to, desperately. I tried to forget about the soft look in his eye. Forget about the warmth of his hands on my arms, pulling me close. Forget about how we almost kissed. How I thought for one stupid moment that he might actually like me.

He stared at me for a while, like he was trying to figure me out, dissect the thoughts inside my head. *Well, good luck*, I wanted to say. I barely knew what I was thinking, much less feeling. When Carson and I were apart, everything became clear again, like staring down into the surf once the seafoam dissolved and the water cleared. I knew what we were, the lines were clearly drawn. But lately, when I was with him...the line blurred. The surf made everything hazy, and I was tangled up in knots, unsure of what we were anymore. Enemies no longer seemed to fit.

We stayed silent on the drive to The Bean. Once we arrived, it was a brief stop. We gathered up the waiting presents people had bought and dropped off, along with a handful of snowflake tags that had gone unclaimed. Then we headed for the Sweet Water Outlets to do our shopping.

Carson pulled into the parking lot of the strip mall. We sat in the car for a moment, and I grew edgy in the silence. It was clear we wouldn't discuss the party since I blew it off, but the arguing outside my house was another issue. I had no clue whether to address it. It felt a bit like the proverbial elephant in the room, and I almost wished for our usual fighting. Arguing with Carson and picking on him might somehow help to ease this ever-present ache in my chest.

I glanced over at him, having no idea what was going through his head as he stared out the windshield in the silence. I half expected him to make a joke of it. But he didn't. Instead, he turned to me, his expression serious. "I thought of some other things we should get for the families."

I practically sighed in relief. He wasn't dwelling on my parent's fighting, so why should I? "Really?"

"Yeah. I think it's great that we're getting the kids clothes and stuff, but I think we need to make sure there are just as many toys. I mean, the clothes are a necessity, but this is probably one of the only times a year they get things they want, not just things they need."

I felt a smile slide its way onto my face. "I agree."

"And I think we should get each family new towels and dishrags. I was even thinking about some new sheets. I actually called Mrs. Parks and got bed sizes for the families."

A wave of shame washed over me. There I was mulling over my own issues, while Carson was thinking of others. People who had less than I did, who had more significant problems than their parents feuding. "Linens like that are expensive though," I said, not wanting to be negative, but knowing with all the other things we needed to purchase there probably wasn't enough in the budget.

"Not too expensive when you received an Addington donation." Carson wiggled his brows. "We could buy sheets for days. I even think we can get each family a gift card."

My eyes widened. "Really?"

Carson nodded. "I may have spoken with Lucas' dad."

"Wow. That's amazing. And I think that's a fabulous idea." I stared at him a moment, my gaze flickering over his face, and when he smiled, his whole face lit up.

"What?" he asked.

"Nothing." I shook my head and glanced away, then peeked at him again from the corner of my eye.

Carson laughed. "What's that look for?"

I picked at the chipping pink polish on my thumbnail. "Nothing. I just. . .I'm surprised."

"What? That I put effort into this?"

"Well, yeah," I said, laughing.

"It was the least I could do. You budgeted out the groceries to the last penny and made all those lists of yours. Plus, you've been picking up the stuff from the Angel Tree on and off, which is so much harder for me with swim practice."

"I suppose," I said, though I wasn't entirely

convinced. Carson actually seemed to care, while I had just been going through the motions, too consumed with my own problems. "You're different than I thought."

His eyes met mine. "How so?"

"You're nice."

We both laughed at that, then I leaned my head back against the seat. The truth was, I thought I had Carson Brooks all figured out. Mr. Carefree, go-with-the-flow, life of the party had a lot more layers to him. Maybe I had been all wrong about him. Perhaps I never really knew him. And if I was wrong, maybe Olivia was wrong too, and he didn't feel sorry for me.

"It's kind of fun surprising you," Carson said, interrupting my thoughts.

I shot him a sidelong glance even as my heart leapt. His dark hair hung in his eyes, and his full lips curved into a grin.

"Carson?" I asked.

"Yeah?"

We both stared straight out into the parking lot as if looking at each other might somehow break this truce—the moment of honesty—we had going.

"Why are you being so nice to me?"

I heard him swallow, and the soft sound of

his breath as his breathing grew shallow. "I've always been nice to you."

I was too tired to scoff, so instead, I just shook my head. "We both know that's not true. Neither of us have been nice," I admitted.

The silence that followed stretched on so long I thought he might not answer, then he said, "Don't you think we're a little old for the fighting? We both leave for college at the end of the summer. We're eighteen. We've had nine years of fighting. I don't want to fight anymore."

"Because?"

You like me. I wanted him to say it—urged him to say the words. And that desire both frightened and excited me because it was so full of possibility.

"Because I want to be your friend."

The air rushed out of my lungs, and for a moment, I wanted to argue with him. To ask him what all those moments at his party were about. Why he seemed particularly interested in whether or not Ethan and I had anything beyond friendship. Why he said he wanted to kiss me, then seemed angry at the thought of me kissing Ethan. I didn't imagine what happened between us in the kitchen. I couldn't have. Yet, I couldn't trust myself where Carson was concerned. Our past indicated that all those things didn't matter. Of course he wanted to be friends.

When his sharp blue eyes met mine, I felt like an idiot for even thinking otherwise. I hated myself for it because that was just one more way Carson Brooks had won.

Reaching across me, Carson opened the glovebox and pulled out a piece of paper I recognized as the list I made.

His hand brushed my arm for the briefest of moments, and I suppressed the shiver it caused.

"Ready?" he asked.

We took our third cartful of items to the car. Stuffed inside the back of Carson's Jeep was everything to make Christmas special. Toys for the kids, clothes, new pajamas, books. We even found a fantastic deal on towels and sheets for each family.

All in all, it had been a good trip. The added donations Carson procured went a long way. If one good thing came out of our punishment, it was that these adopted families of Sweet Water would have an amazing Christmas.

At least someone would. This knowledge made the sting of my own crappy holiday somewhat bearable.

"Last stop," Carson said.

"Yes. Let's do this." My feet ached, and I was starving.

As we headed toward the perfume shop, I said, "I think it's kind of cute that some of the people from the nursing home requested perfume and cologne."

"It just goes to show that you're never too old to take pride in yourself. Why shouldn't they smell good, too? When I'm an old geezer, I plan on rocking some Oakleys and the latest Gucci scent. I'll be pimpin' it till the day I die. All the old ladies will be swooning at my feet."

I snorted. "Dropping like flies at the bottom of your wheelchair's more like it."

Carson grinned. "Hey, whatever works. I'll have my own private room. I'll scoop 'em up and wheel them back to my pad."

I couldn't help but laugh at the image. "You're sick, you know that?"

"I've been called worse things," he said with a wink. No doubt those things had been uttered by yours truly.

After entering the shop, we headed towards the displays of perfume. "What all do we have to get?" I asked.

Carson consulted his paper. "Four bottles of perfume and two bottles of cologne."

"Perfume is such an individualized thing. I wish they had written down specifics. What if we get something they hate?" I asked.

"We'll have to choose wisely, but I have impeccable taste, so..."

I arched a brow at him. "Full of ourselves, are we?"

Carson shrugged and glanced at me, grinning. "Hey, can't fight the truth, baby. Besides, you always smell terrific, so I'm sure that won't happen."

My pulse skipped. The words left his lips so smoothly, and so quickly, I wasn't sure I really heard them. "You think I smell good?" I wanted to shove the question back in, but it was too late. They were out there in all my insecure glory for him to hear.

He shrugged like it was nothing. "Yeah, of course." He scanned the perfume selections. Picking one up, he sniffed it and grimaced, then set it back down. "Your scent...it's amazing, like a combination of coconut, vanilla frosting, and something floral, but I don't know what."

Freesia. The floral is freesia.

I inhaled a ragged breath. Carson Brooks thinks I smell good.

Needing something to do with my hands, I reached for the nearest bottle of perfume and handed it to him. "What about this one?"

He took a step closer and leaned in, smelling it before he broke out into a fit of coughing. "Oh, my gosh. I think my sinuses might be bleeding."

"Hmm, really? I was thinking of buying it for myself," I teased.

"Don't you dare." With a serious expression, he snatched the bottle from my hands and put it back on the shelf.

"So, that's a no?"

"A hard no," he said, grinning.

Next, I picked up a pink bottle shaped like a flower and took a whiff. The scent made me want to puke. It was perfect. Holding it out, I said, "This one's really nice."

"Let me see." He narrowed his eyes on me as if he suspected it was a trick and inhaled. His eyes instantly watered, and he fake-gagged. "Man, that's bad. It's like a rose massacre. The smell of nightmares."

For the next thirty minutes, it became a game, each of us choosing the worst scents we could possibly find. Nothing was off limits, and the object was to one-up each other. Who could find the most hideous perfume. When I found a dark blue bottle of cologne called Poison Dart, I chuckled to myself. I had this in the bag. No way a cologne with the word poison in it smelled good.

When Carson came to test my selection, I plucked his t-shirt off his chest and spritzed him with it.

"Hey!" He tipped his head down and grimaced. "Oh, man." He choked. "I think they successfully bottled the smell of death. What's this one called?"

"Poison Dart."

"Yup. That's about right. You win, and I concede. Poison Dart definitely takes the bag. Worst cologne ever."

I laughed so hard, my stomach ached.

"You owe me big time," he said, then before I could stop him, he reached out and yanked me toward him. Pulling me into his arms, he wrapped them around me, engulfing me in a cloud of the odorous stench. "How do you like it?" he asked.

I struggled to break free from his vice grip, but when my eyes met his, I stilled. They were so close I could make out every minute detail. "Your eyes have little flecks of green in them," I rasped. It must be why they sometimes looked aqua in the light.

"Thanks for noticing." He smirked, and I shoved at his chest, then moved out from under his arm.

"Can I help you two with something?" A woman's voice said.

I glanced over my shoulder to see a Perfume Mania employee, wearing a carefully controlled smile. I imagine she must've grown tired of our antics and wanted to make a sale.

My heart drummed in my chest as I caught sight of the goofy look on Carson's face. God, he was cute sometimes. And he knew it too, which made admitting it all that much harder.

"Are we trying to find a scent for your girl-friend?" The woman asked, startling me from my daze.

My cheeks burned. *Did she just call me his girlfriend?*

"Yes," Carson answered, grinning playfully. Then he stepped closer and wrapped his arms around me from behind and squeezed.

Butterflies rioted in my stomach as the warmth of his chest met my back. He was jok-ing, messing around. He thought it was funny the saleswoman had mistaken us for a couple. And I supposed it was. Just the idea of Carson and I to-gether was hilarious.

But I wasn't laughing. Though my head knew it was a joke, my body said otherwise. My heart jumped into my throat, and my mouth turned to sand.

"But only the best for my girl. I want the perfect fragrance. What do you recommend?" he asked, deadpan, and gave my arms a little squeeze.

The woman prattled on about her theory on perfume, while Carson nodded, hanging onto every word. Meanwhile, the synapses in my brain were firing at warp speed. All I could think about was how this is what it would be like, to be Carson's girl, for real.

It was strange how I could picture it so clearly. How easy and natural the image of us together felt in my head. We'd go out and laugh and joke. He'd make me forget all my problems like today—my parents, my college applications, the dance, all the things that sucked about going back home. And when his arms would wrap around me, I'd go weak. Everything else in my life would be a blur because the warmth of his arms, the cut of his smile were all that mattered.

". . .so, you see, the best perfumes are meant to compliment the person. Why don't you describe your girlfriend?" The saleswoman said, snapping me out of my thoughts. "Her personality, everything about her," she added.

My insides clenched. "Oh, that won't be necessary," I said.

"Nonsense," the saleswoman said. "No one can accurately describe the way others see them. Who better to judge than your boyfriend?"

Oh, yes, who better? I could think of a few.

I trained my eyes on the floor, allowing my mortification to sink into my bones. With any luck, I could just disappear—poof!—into thin air.

Carson nudged me in the arm. "Yeah, Mia. Who better than your sexy and devastatingly handsome boyfriend?"

I chuckled, his joke allowing me to glance back at him and roll my eyes, play it off like my heart wasn't threatening to beat out of my chest.

"How to describe Mia Randalls..." Carson's voice trailed off, and I squeezed my eyes shut, fighting the urge to twist around in his arms and cover his mouth with my hands. I wanted to stop him. Because suddenly this didn't seem like a joke anymore. It was personal, and I wasn't sure I could bear to hear what he had to say—to see myself through his eyes.

"She's smart, but it's not just that she's smart. She works harder than anyone I know, yet she's too hard on herself. Everyone likes Mia. From the geeks to the jocks to the stoners, every single group of kids in our class has nothing but the best to say about her because she never judges. She's not petty like other people. She doesn't gossip, but instead, she gives people the benefit of the doubt. I've seen her put others first, one too many times because she hates confrontation. Unless it's with me, of course, and then she's brutal."

Carson's voice grew soft as he turned me around in his arms to face him. "But she puts too much pressure on herself to be perfect. And I hate that. It eats away at me when I see it."

My heart pounded like a drum in my chest until I thought it might burst. All I could do was stare up at him, my lashes fluttering as I blinked away my shock.

He reached up to my hair and smoothed a hand through my locks, and for a moment, I wondered if he remembered we weren't alone, that there was someone—a stranger—standing only feet away from us, but he just continued, dragging his fingers through the length of my locks as he said, "Her hair. . .it reminds me of the sunset—both orange, and fiery pink, and pale yellow at the same time. She's a good friend—loyal to the core and trustworthy, the kind who will be on your side through anything. And her laugh. . .She has this laugh. The one where she doesn't think someone's funny, but she's pretending anyway. That laugh doesn't reach her eyes. But her real laugh, now that's something to see because her whole face gets into it. It's uncontrollable. It sounds like wind chimes, and she crinkles her nose and eyes."

Reaching up, he touched the bridge of my nose, making me gasp. "And every time I hear it, I think, I want to be the one to make her laugh like that because it's impossible to hear and not smile. It pulls you in, that laugh."

Breathing became a struggle as he grew silent, staring down at me, his mouth a tight line as his eyes searched mine. I wanted to say something—anything—but the words were stuck in my throat. The things he said about me, they didn't sound like observations of a boy who loathed me. Quite the contrary.

"Well," the saleswoman breathed, "then we need something extraordinary. Hold on a moment." She breezed past me, toward shelves at the back. But I barely noticed. I hardly noticed anything except the boy in front of me.

And every time I hear it, I think, I want to be the one to make her laugh like that... His words were a sucker punch. They formed a lump in my throat and left me disoriented. I wasn't entirely sure what just happened, but I could feel the floor shift underneath us. Something had changed.

But before I could say anything, the woman was back, holding out a small crystal-shaped bottle with an amber liquid inside. I watched dumbly as she took my arm and spritzed some on the insides of my wrist, and over my clavicle as Carson's gaze tracked her movements like a lion watching his prey.

"Try this," she murmured, then stepped back, giving Carson room.

And before I could prepare myself and process what was happening, he stepped forward, bending down, his face inches from my neck. The warmth of his skin radiated off of him. His lower lips grazed the spot where my pulse pounded. And as he breathed me in, he hummed in response. The sound made my heart skip, made my hands sweat. It was single handedly the most sensual thing that had happened to me in my eighteen years on this earth. And when he pulled away from me and took a step back, I felt a regret so strong, so deep, it made my heart hurt.

His eyes met mine, his breathing heavy. "Yep. That's definitely the one."

CHAPTER ELEVEN

C arson drove us to Luigi's in silence. Every so often, I stole a glance at him, but when he turned his gaze to mine, I looked away. His words kept replaying in my head. I couldn't forget them if I tried, and all I could think was that for someone who was supposed to be my enemy, it certainly seemed he knew a lot about me. Despite our years of feuding, he'd been paying attention. And that thought made me feel all warm and tingly inside, like someone lit a firecracker in my heart.

And the only thing more confusing and frightening than the possibility of Carson having feelings for me was the notion that I think I liked him too.

When he pulled into Luigi's and parked, he turned to me. "Okay, what's up?" he asked. "You've been super quiet this whole ride."

"Oh. Um, it's nothing," I said, but my voice was two octaves too high.

He arched a brow like he didn't believe me. "You hungry?"

I nodded and bit my lip. Suddenly, I forgot how to use my voice.

He grinned, then shook his head and got out of the Jeep, rounding the front until he reached my side and opened my door. The sunlight caught his hair, turning it bronze as he reached out his hand for me, and even though this was the same boy that once put grass in my peanut butter sandwich, everything seemed brand new. Different.

He clasped my hand in his, warm and confident, then led us inside. The wait was short, and the entire time, he held my hand as his other one played with a lock of my hair, while I stood immobile, afraid to move for the fear that I'd break this spell and he'd stop.

Once we settled into a booth, Carson sat across from me and leaned his forearms onto the table. He filled every available space with his broad shoulders, his long arms, and his confident smile. "Thanks for spending the afternoon with me," he said like we had a choice and it wasn't for the Angel Program. "What would you have done had I not shown up?"

Gone insane? Filed divorce papers for *my parents? Languished inside my room all day until Ethan called?* All of those were viable options. "Probably more of what I was doing when you knocked on my door."

"Which was?"

I exhaled. "Drown myself in music so loud nothing else existed." It'd be a miracle if I had eardrums left by graduation.

Carson's smile tightened. "What's going on with your parents?" When I didn't answer right away, he continued, "You don't have to tell me if you don't want to. I know—"

"So you heard them, huh?" I asked, then I closed my eyes. "What am I saying? Of course you heard them. How could you not?" I mumbled.

"How long have they been doing that?"

"They didn't always fight like that." I stared off into space, remembering a time when things were different—better. "They used to be this perfect couple."

Kinda like your parents. I swallowed and barely met Carson's gaze before glancing away again.

"Tell me about it," he said, his voice soft.

I hesitated as the past rushed in, reminding

me it was Carson sitting across from me. But he was different with me now. There was a tenderness to his voice, all of the things he said in the perfume shop, the thought and care he put into the Angel Program for people he didn't even know, and I thought, yeah, *this* is Carson. He's not the boy you thought he was. He's so much more—someone I could trust, maybe even rely on.

"It's been a couple years. But it's been getting a lot worse these last six months, since the start of the school year." I paused and chewed on my lip for a moment, wondering how much I should tell him. "It's been pretty bad. Stressful is an understatement. Pretty much every day in my house is a war zone, one I want no part of."

"That must be hard," he said, and I could tell he meant it. His voice, his eyes, they were so full of sincerity it hurt.

I swallowed the lump in my throat. "Most days, I put my headphones on and blast my music to drown them out. Going to your house to hang out with Ethan is pretty much the only thing keeping me sane. My house is a battleground, and yours is my refuge." My voice cracked, so I took a calming breath.

"What do they fight about?"

"Anything. Everything." I laughed. "I mean, I'm sure there was a starting point, some catalyst to set everything in motion. I'm pretty sure my mom thinks my dad cheated with his assistant. I have no idea if it's true or not, or if it's just a convenient excuse to fuel their feud. It doesn't really matter what started it anymore though because they find something worth arguing about every day. If my mom says the sky is blue, my dad argues it's indigo."

I glanced up at him as I toyed with the straw in my ice water, eyeing him from beneath my lashes. Why was I telling him all of this?

"You know, when we got in trouble for the gym incident, they were mad at me for half a second before they turned on each other. Each of them blamed the other for my getting in trouble at school. Isn't that crazy? I could wind up stumbling home drunk or wreck my car, and they'd each have a finger to point. It's like I'm no longer even there. It's just them all the time and this anger between them. It lives and breathes in the walls."

"Is that why you want out so bad? To go to Duke, I mean. Is that why you're desperate for early admission?"

I offered him a small smile. "Yes and no."

"Explain."

"At first, it started as wanting something to celebrate, a piece of good news that might somehow glue us back together. Any early admission would do, even though Duke was always my number one. So I applied to a handful of good early admissions programs. I thought that if I could get in somewhere, anywhere, then they would be proud of me. They would have something to be happy about, like that could somehow fix us. But lately, I see more and more just how stupid that is. There's nothing that'll fix them now."

Something flickered through Carson's eyes as he gripped my hand, tracing small, slow circles with his thumb. "It's not stupid at all. You're human. And you care. You want to help, but you feel at a loss, so you're grasping at whatever you think might make a difference. It's not fair, but it's not stupid."

I swallowed over the lump in my throat. "Now I just want to get away. Is that terrible of me? To want to just disappear?"

"No."

The way he said it, so firm and strong, made me believe it.

To my horror, my eyes filled with tears, so I blinked them back. "They're going to get divorced. I know it. Heck, I want them to, just so all the fighting will stop, but at the same time, I don't think I can bear to see it. It's the end of something so huge. I don't know how I'd adjust to that, but having the buffer between Sweet Water and Duke would help. Maybe it won't seem so bad then—when I'm away. Maybe separate holidays and splitting time won't hurt quite so much either."

Reaching up, Carson tucked a lock of hair behind my ear, and I wanted nothing more than to sink into his touch. Nothing had felt so right in a long time. I don't know what gave me the courage to tell him everything. Maybe it was knowing he actually cared, but speaking my truth released something inside me. And no matter what came of us, whether we returned to being enemies after the holidays or remained friends—or whatever this was—for this time, this moment, now, I was thankful.

"So how will Christmas be, at your house?"

I worried my lip with my teeth. It was a good question. There hadn't been much mention of the holidays. "I don't know," I answered honestly. Then I shrugged. "I'll probably sit at home and watch movies. We don't even have a tree up."

Emotion swelled in my throat. The last thing I wanted to do was cry, so I spoke through the sting of threatening tears, willing them away. "I'm sure my parents will do something. Even if it's not the same, it'll be okay. I'll bake some cookies and put some music on," I said, with false cheer, because really, I felt like doing none of those things.

"You should come to our place for Christmas," Carson said. "You know my parents love you, right? I think they secretly hope either Ethan or I end up with you one day. You're like the daughter they never had. They'd love to have you there, trust me."

I felt myself blush. The idea of being with Carson. . .

I smiled, feeling suddenly shy, and glanced away. "Yeah, maybe. I should probably spend the morning with my parents, but I'm sure I could come over. I'd love that, actually." The thought of being with a family that actually wanted to be together sounded pretty nice.

"Mia. . ." Carson touched the side of my cheek, turning my gaze toward him. "Come to my meet on Saturday."

"Like, with Ethan?"

Carson glanced down to the table then back again, lifting a shoulder. "With Ethan, or alone. Alone is good." He laughed, and it was maybe the first and only time I'd heard him sound nervous. "I want you to come watch me swim. Will you?"

Out of all the words he just said, the words, *I want you,* were the three I focused on. Why did they sound so good coming from him? Why did they make my heart soar and my insides twist?

I'm in trouble, I thought. Totally hopeless. And as Carson gazed at me intently from across the table, my heart sped up. There was no way I'd say no. "Okay, I'd like that."

A moment later, the waitress came to the table to take our order, apologizing for the wait, and I thought, *take all the time you want*. Then I realized with a little pull inside my chest that if there was one thing I learned these last weeks about Carson, it was how impossible he was to resist.

Tuesday morning, I woke early and padded my way into the kitchen, rubbing the sleep from my eyes. Sunlight streamed through the windows helping to clear the haze of sleep. When I headed to the refrigerator and yanked open the door, my mom appeared in the entryway.

"Hey, Mia."

"Mom," I acknowledged, bending over and searching for something worth eating.

"What do you say we go grab breakfast. Just you and me?"

I turned toward her and closed the fridge door. Going to breakfast was Mom's code for: I want to talk to you about something serious. So, I searched her face, looking for a hint of what was in store for me.

The hair on my arms prickled. "Where's Dad?" I asked.

"Already at work." She smiled weakly, then said, "Come on. Go get dressed. It'll be fun. We'll go to Sweet Water Stacks."

Sweet Water Stacks was a bribe. She knew it was my favorite because they served waffles two inches thick, stacked three-high, with fruit and whipped cream.

My hesitation was brief before I said, "Okay," and hurried out of the kitchen and up the stairs, but not without a lump in my throat and a sinking in my gut.

By the time we arrived at the little diner, the silence in the car was deafening. We were seated almost immediately, and after we placed our orders, Mom curled her hands around her coffee cup, and I knew it was coming. Whatever her reason for wanting to talk, I was about to find out. "I want to apologize. I know I haven't been around much lately, or at least not very present."

I swallowed. So this was about her and Dad. It's what I expected. Still, that didn't make it any easier.

I played with the silverware in front of me, rubbing at the hard water marks and buffing it out until I could see my reflection in my spoon. "Neither has Dad," I pointed out, mostly because saying something felt better than staying quiet.

Mom nodded and bit her lower lip before meeting my eyes again. "I just want you to know that you're a good kid, Mia. You've always made things so easy." She smiled again, and for a moment, I just wished she'd stop. It was brittle and weak and fake, and I wanted no false happiness from her. It only reminded me of how wrong everything was.

While I was old enough to rationalize that none of this was my fault—her and Dad—her comment only reminded me of how I may have been an easy kid, but it wasn't enough to hold our family together. Maybe nothing was.

"What's happening with you guys?" I asked. "Are you going to get a divorce?"

"I don't know."

Well, at least she wasn't lying.

Mom refilled her coffee cup from the little carafe on the table, and I sensed it was more to keep her hands busy than anything. Then she took a sip and glanced up at me. "Whatever happens, we love you. I want you to know that. And everything will be okay."

The way she said it made me think she did know what was going to happen with them. Maybe she was lying after all. Then again, I already knew what the future held. It was only a matter of time before they split. Part of me wondered why they didn't just get it over with. Like ripping a Band-Aid off. Instead, they were slowly picking away at the scab, and all it did was make it bleed until it was sure to leave a scar.

Mom reached out and squeezed my hand over the cheap gingham tablecloth, and I tried to focus on the bright red and white squares, but it was hard through the blur of tears.

"You've done nothing wrong in this, Mia. Nothing. You've been amazing, and what's happening between your father and I is between us. It's on us. We've grown apart. Things have happened. Maybe we got too comfortable and stopped trying. Maybe that was the problem. I don't know that it's as simple as one thing or one reason that's torn us down, but you, my dear, are the one amazing thing that came from us. And we will never regret that. We could never regret you. Ever."

By the time we arrived home from breakfast, a heaviness had settled on my shoulders. I was pretty sure Mom's talk was supposed to reassure me, but it somehow made me all the more anxious. At any second, my world could be flipped upside down.

I just wished they'd get it over with.

I hopped out of the car and walked next to my mom to the front door. A large box sat on the front porch. Taped to the top of it was a card with my name on it, written in the small, sloppy scrawl I recognized as Carson's handwriting.

"What's this?" Mom said, picking up the card.

I yanked it from her hands, then blushed. "Sorry. Um, I think it's from Carson."

"Brooks?" Her eyes widened, conveying her surprise.

Welcome to the club.

"Uh, yeah," I said, avoiding her gaze.

She crossed her arms in front of her chest. "Oh. So, how's the Angel Program going? Good, I take it?"

"Yeah, good." I nodded. My fingers itched to open the box. All I wanted to do was take it up to my room so I could see what was inside.

"Good," Mom repeated like it was a new word. "Well, I'm glad," she said with a knowing smile. "You know, I always thought he might have a crush on you. When you guys were kids, he used to watch you and Ethan at the beach playing. He was always trying to get your attention."

I grinned. To think all these years, all I had to do to get Carson to stop antagonizing me was to pay him attention.

"Well, go on. I know you're dying to open it." She shooed me inside. "I won't hover."

"Thanks, Mom," I called out as I picked up the box. Then proceeded up the stairs, the box balanced in front of me.

"Don't fall," she hollered after me.

I hurried into my bedroom, set the box down on the floor, and opened the card. Inside was a small note.

> *Mia,*
>
> *You deserve the best. And though the quality of this tree is questionable, it's little like you. Maybe it's kismet.*
>
> *Or maybe it's all the drugstore had left. But everyone deserves a tree. Especially you.*
>
> *Merry Christmas, Shorty.*
>
> *Yours,*
>
> *Carson*

I smiled as I opened the box, and, sure enough, inside was a little two-foot Christmas tree. The pine branches stretched to the top of the box, reaching like little arms. Scooping it up by the plastic base, I pulled it out and set it on top of my desk.

Hanging from the little branches were small plastic bulbs in pink, blue, and silver. Strung across the artificial pine, on clear twine that looked suspiciously like fishing wire, were diamond-shaped crystals. And when I clicked the red button on the box at the base, bright, white lights twinkled like stars.

It was maybe the best tree I'd ever seen. And it was mine.

Sinking down into my desk chair, I stared at it, memorizing every little detail before I picked up my cell and dialed Carson's number to tell him thanks. When he finally answered, and I heard the deep rumble of his voice, my stomach somersaulted, and all I could think was that it felt a lot like falling.

CHAPTER TWELVE

I wiped my damp palms on the top of my jeans and glanced at the people around me, wondering if anyone else could possibly be as nervous as I was.

That morning, I put on my Wild Cats hoodie and a pair of cute jeans, then took a ridiculous amount of time to weave my peachy locks into a fishtail braid underneath a baseball cap. Some light makeup and lip gloss completed the look. All in all, I thought I looked cute, but not like I was trying too hard.

My phone dinged again, but I ignored it, shoving down the little surge of guilt that accompanied that sound. Ethan had texted me just before I left the house, asking if I wanted to hang out. As a general rule, we didn't lie to each other. But something felt wrong about telling him I was going to Carson's meet. And if I'd told him and he wanted to go, then what? Carson made it pretty clear without saying so that he wanted me to come alone.

He wanted me. All to himself. And how could I argue with that?

I wasn't doing anything wrong, I told myself as I waited for Carson's relays. I was allowed to have a life outside of Ethan. Even he had plans to officially ask Beth out over winter break, and then he'd be so preoccupied, I'd hardly see him.

By the time I arrived at the meet, junior varsity had already finished swimming. I sat through girls varsity, and when they finished their final relay, I knew the boys varsity was finally about to start, which meant Carson would be up soon.

I searched for him in the team seats by the pool, but there was no sight of him. It wasn't more than a minute later, however, when I felt a small tug on the messy braid trailing over my shoulder and turned.

Carson smiled at me. "Having fun?"

"Yeah," I said, and I hardly recognized my own voice. It was soft and breathless.

The Wild Cats warm-up suit he wore

brought out the blue in his eyes, and there was an energy there I had never seen before, one that I was sure had to do with the race. As he ran a hand through his messy, dark hair, he laughed. "Liar. I'm sure you're bored."

"Brooks!" His coach yelled from across the pool, where he stood, clipboard in hand.

Carson rolled his eyes. "That man keeps tabs on me like I'm his kid."

"Well, they can't be missing their star swimmer, now can they?"

His eyes glittered, and he slapped a hand to his chest. "Is that a compliment coming from Mia Randalls?"

"Maybe."

"Or is she just flirting with me?" He tapped the underside of my baseball cap, smiling. "I'd better go." Carson grinned as he backed away, watching me the whole time. "Tell Mom I said hi," he hollered, then winked and walked off.

I watched as he made his way to the coach and listened to something he was saying as he undressed, taking off his zip-up jacket first. He stretched his muscular arms, crossing them back and forth across his chest, warming up. All his muscles flickered with the movement, and I was so mesmerized by his washboard stomach, it took me a second to notice he had removed his warm-up pants, revealing the tight Wild Cat swim shorts. Of course Carson took that moment to catch my eye, and his grin turned to a self-satisfied smirk.

Biting my lip, I averted my gaze, even as my cheeks caught fire. Behind me, someone cleared their throat, then tapped me on the shoulder. "Hey, honey. I didn't know you'd be here."

Startled, I glanced to the sound of Mrs. Brooks.

"Oh, hi, Mrs. Brooks."

"What a nice surprise," Mrs. Brooks said as she left her husband to take a seat next to me.

Carson's words registered. *Say hi to my mom.* He had known Mr. and Mrs. Brooks were sitting close by. He wanted them to know I was there, and something about that made me feel special. I wasn't just another friend watching him race.

"I'm so glad we made it. We got stuck behind an accident, serves us right for waiting until varsity was up. Did Carson ask you to come?" She smiled, glancing at her son.

In other words, she was trying to find out if I was there for Carson or someone else. I nodded and smiled, reminding myself they were still Ethan's parents. They liked me. "Yeah."

A glimmer of something passed through her eyes. "That's wonderful, honey." She patted my leg, and I found myself hoping she didn't ask about Ethan. "Your little project must be going well then, huh?" she asked.

"Yeah, it's been kind of fun, actually."

"It's so nice, you two volunteering your time like that."

I smiled, thinking of that day at dinner when Carson and I goaded each other. Clearly, she was never told the truth.

She leaned over and bumped my shoulder. "You know, Carson's always been so fond of you. It's nice to finally see you two spending some time together."

My gaze shifted back to Carson, who was now uber-focused, his attention trained on the water. The first boys relay had started, and Carson didn't waste a second. Instead of relaxing until it was his turn at the podium, he studied the other swimmers as they raced.

The next thirty minutes passed quickly with me squeezing Mrs. Brooks' hand as Carson swam. He competed in two relays in which he won and stood on the block, waiting for the starting call of his final race.

He positioned himself, still as stone. And when the starting gun sounded, he propelled himself into the water, clearing nearly half the pool with just one dive. He kicked his legs like a fish until he began to surface, gliding through the clear blue, before using his arms.

Muscle glistened as his long arm strokes propelled him. He gained a small lead after the first lap. His movements were smooth, effortless, his kick turns faster than any I'd ever seen, and as I watched him, it made me wish I could swim like that, be so good at something.

He was almost a foot ahead of a kid from Cedar Creek—the closest thing to competition in this event. The others were far behind, and when he approached the wall again and turned with ease, kicking his feet until he surfaced, then used his arms again, he increased his lead twice fold.

Beside us, Mr. Brooks held his phone in his hands, checking it. "I think he's going to break his record," he murmured.

My stomach clenched, saying a silent prayer for him, while Mrs. Brooks squealed and squeezed my arm, and before I knew what I was doing, I was on my feet, clapping and cheering, screaming with a few others in the crowd.

His lead increased further. He was a torpedo in the water, now nearly two body-lengths ahead of the other swimmers, and when he slapped the wall, he shoved his goggles up, his gaze immediately shifting needle-sharp to the digital clock on the wall. Then he slapped a hand in the water and raised his fist in the air.

"He did it!" Mrs. Brooks bounced to her feet beside me. "He beat his record and the Sweet Valley record for the 200-meter!"

As the other swimmers finished, Carson turned, his gaze automatically finding mine in the crowd, and he grinned. Around me, people cheered or filed out of the bleachers, bumping me on their way down. But I just stood there, my gaze caught on his, transfixed by the rise and fall of Carson's chest as he caught his breath, frozen by the warmth of his smile. And all I could think was, *I'm completely and irrevocably screwed.*

We fell over the doorstep of the Brooks' home laughing. I smacked Carson on the arm, wiping the tears from my eyes. "Shut up. I did not!"

"You totally did. When Olivia stopped by our table, you definitely gave her the evil eye. But that's okay. It's kinda hot, having you jealous."

Glaring, I placed my hands on my hips as Carson laughed, but I couldn't really even be mad. After the race, a bunch of kids from school stopped by the Burger Bar for burgers and shakes, where Carson continued to surprise me. He was funny, engaging, and attentive. Even though we were with his swimming buddies, he held my hand the entire time, always making sure I was okay. Even when Olivia showed up and stopped by our table, he continued to dote on me, despite her attempts at flirting. And, okay, I'd admit it. I may have gotten a little territorial. But, really, did that girl ever quit?

"What's so funny?"

I whirled around at the sound of Ethan's voice.

He stood at the bottom of the stairs, one hand resting on the knoll post, while his gaze flickered between us.

I glanced guiltily up to Carson like I got caught in a lie, which wasn't entirely inaccurate. I had planned on texting Ethan back, but I got so distracted after the race, I forgot.

"Oh, um, hey," I said, giving him an awkward wave.

Ethan crossed his arms over his chest, and before I could explain, Carson said, "Inside joke."

Ethan's eyes flashed, then returned to mine. "Mom said you went to Carson's meet."

My insides shrunk at the angry look in his eye. "Yeah, I did," I said, playing with the sleeve of my jacket, hating that I felt so weird about this.

"His party Saturday, shopping Monday, dinner, his swim meet, and now lunch at the Burger Bar? Sounds like more than just the Angel Program at work."

Carson straightened, his tone hard when he said, "What's your point?" Then he turned to me and grabbed my hand. "Come on, Mia, you don't have to explain yourself to him."

I swallowed, torn between the two boys when Ethan shrugged. "No point. I'm just making an observation."

Carson met my eye, waiting for me to say something. But what? Did he want me to go with him? Ethan was my best friend. I couldn't just blow him off completely.

When Ethan cocked his head, he asked, "Are we still going to Sweet Surf to catch their sale on boards, Mia?"

Oh crap. I forgot.

Taking my hesitation as a rejection, he scoffed. "I guess you were going to do that with Carson too."

"She'd probably have more fun," Carson said under his breath. Ethan mustn't have heard him, though because he kept his eyes laser-focused on me.

"Of course, I'm going," I said, crossing my arms over my chest, feeling a little defensive and annoyed he was so gruff.

"*And* that's my cue," Carson drawled. "I'm out." He saluted Ethan, which earned him a death-stare before he turned back to me.

Leaning in close, he placed one hand on my waist, and I sucked in a breath, as his fingertips burned through the thin cotton of my shirt. Then in a move so slow, so smooth and calculated, he bent down and brushed his lips over my cheek, a whisper-soft kiss that made me shiver and shot butterflies through my belly, yearning for the real thing.

"I'll see you tomorrow?" he asked. "We'll put the baskets together?"

I nodded my agreement, because I couldn't speak, not with Ethan's penetrating gaze burning a hole through the side of my face. Not without the feel of Carson's lips still on my skin. And then he turned and bounded up the stairs, past Ethan, who watched him go, his eyes narrowed on his back, knife-sharp before he turned to me.

I swallowed, finding enough strength to offer him a genuine smile through the pounding of my heart. "Ready to go?" I asked.

As we pulled out of the driveway three minutes later, I found myself wishing I were still inside—with Carson. Only my gaze flickered to the upstairs window, to where I saw his shadow, highlighted by the glow of the light from within, and I turned to Ethan and smiled, acting like everything was okay. Like he was still my world, my best friend, even though I'd rather be with his brother.

CHAPTER THIRTEEN

The remainder of my week consisted of days spent with Ethan and evenings spent organizing supplies with Carson. Time split between two Brooks boys. I spent far more time at their house than my own. Whether or not my parents noticed, I had no idea. I hadn't spent enough time there to care.

Ethan lay back in his bed, tossing a football up in the air, while I sat at his desk chair, filling out a college application. "Which school is that for again?" he asked.

"Purdue."

Ethan grunted. "You haven't even heard back from Duke yet."

"I know. But I can't just wait around and do nothing. I might as well start getting other applications ready in case I don't get early acceptance."

A knock on the door interrupted us. I turned, and my eyes locked with Carson's as he leaned inside the doorway, his damp hair framing his face from his late-day swim. A ball of heat curled in my belly and a slow smiled curved my lips.

"Hey, you ready to get packing the last of the stuff? Mom and Dad went to dinner, but they ordered pizza for us. You game?"

"Definitely." I put my paperwork down and stood.

Ethan scowled. "So you can stop what you're doing for him?" Then he checked his watch. "It's only five o'clock, and you guys were gone all afternoon shopping. Can't it wait?"

I shifted on my feet, wishing he'd just make this easy on me and let me go. "Well, this is the last day. We have to organize everything into care packages for the families. Tomorrow, we meet Mrs. Parks, then we do the grocery shopping and deliver everything," I said.

"Right. I get it," Ethan said, turning his attention away from us.

He didn't look like he got it.

"Don't be mad." I nudged him in the arm.

"We'll come and grab you after we're finished," I said, realizing much too late my use of the word "we."

Ethan, however, hadn't missed it. His head snapped up, and he arched a brow in question. After, he shook his head and grumbled as he began tossing the football in the air again.

"We can go to the late showing of that movie you wanted to see," I added.

"Whatever. Have fun."

And though I felt guilty, I left his room and joined Carson downstairs.

An hour later, Carson and I had effectively demolished a whole pepperoni pizza—okay, I ate two pieces while Carson all but inhaled the rest—and we had basically taken over the living room.

"You'll have to thank your mom for all the boxes if I don't see her tonight. These are perfect." I lugged a box of presents to the corner of the finished baskets and wrote the family's name on it in marker. "And for letting us take over the place," I added, surveying the mess. The floor was covered.

I pulled a face, and we both laughed, something we found ourselves doing quite often.

Carson caught my eye, and I allowed my gaze flicker to his mouth, wondering if he'd try to kiss me. Part of me felt like I've waited forever.

He cleared his throat and glanced away

again, his cheeks turning pink. "Well, it's only for two more days. This stuff will be out of here soon enough."

"What all do we have left to do tonight?" I asked, checking the master list. "Looks like we just need to divvy up the wrapping paper and gift bags so that the parents can wrap the kids' gifts, then we'll be done. Gosh, it's going to take a million trips to deliver all this stuff. We don't even have the food yet."

Carson shrugged. "Nah. It won't be that bad. We'll have my Jeep. And I can skip practice in the morning."

"Carson Brooks is going to skip his morning swim practice?" My eyes widened as I teased. I clutched at my chest like I might have a heart attack. "Someone alert the press. Call the Sweet Water Gazette STAT!"

"Haha. Funny."

I jabbed him in the ribs, and he grabbed my hand, playfully tugging me forward. Once I was right in front of him, he brushed a lock of hair from my eyes, and I thought, *This is it*. Then he attacked my ribs with his fingers.

"No!" I screamed, breathless. "No. No. No."

"Oh, someone's ticklish," he crowed, laughing.

His fingers moved lightly over my ribs and

my back as I squirmed in his arms, laughing until my stomach hurt. "Stop," I begged.

"Not until you say please."

"Puh-lease," I wheezed.

He stopped but made no effort to move his arms. Instead, he kept them wrapped around me, my back pressed into the warmth of his chest, and everything inside me came alive. My heart knocked against my rib cage, my breathing quickened, and my palms dampened. Suddenly, my senses heightened. I could smell the shampoo in his hair, feel the warmth of his breath on my neck. Blood pounded in my ears as his fingers gripped my waist and slowly turned me.

"Hey," he said, his voice husky. His eyes scanned my face, landing on my mouth.

"Hey," I whispered. And then his mouth was on mine, warm and soft, and everything I thought it'd be.

His long arms tightened around me, pulling me further into his chest as he lifted me slightly off my feet, and I thought, this is what a kiss should be like. All other kisses before this one had been a waste, just practice for the main event. Because nothing compared to kissing Carson Brooks.

He angled his head, guiding my lips apart, deepening the kiss as a little sigh escaped my mouth. His lips teased and coaxed. He nipped my lower lip, then kissed me harder, his tongue brushing mine, and I wondered idly where he learned to kiss like this, then decided I didn't want to know.

Dragging his fingertips up my arms, leaving goosebumps in their wake, he slid them into my hair, angling my head, both of us sinking into the kiss further—a tangle of lips and limbs and breathless sighs until my stomach tightened and everything inside me burned, a fire ripping through me from the inside out.

When he pulled away slightly, he helped me find my footing, his breathing heavy. Then he swallowed and stared into my eyes. "Mia, I was wondering. . .I wanted to ask you if—"

"Mia, are you finished yet?" Ethan's voice boomed, startling us apart. I jumped, and Carson's arms fell away, back to his sides.

My cheeks burned guiltily as Ethan entered the room, eyeing both of us strangely. "You ready?" he asked, his tone clipped.

"What? To go where?" I blinked through the haze of confusion, the kiss having killed a couple thousand brain cells, thinking it was a miracle I could even speak.

"The movie? You said we could go to the late showing. Remember? If we're going to make it, we need to leave now."

"Oh, uh." I glanced back to the boxes, then

to Carson. How did I tell him I'd rather stay there and pack boxes with his brother? And okay, maybe I wanted to kiss him again, to see if we could recreate the moment we just shared or if it was a one-time fluke. I was betting it wasn't a fluke.

"Forget it." Ethan shook his head, obviously sensing my hesitation, his shoulders tense.

Carson stepped forward, grabbing the bag of wrapping paper, and catching my eye. "It's cool. You guys go. I'll finish up."

My stomach sunk. "You sure? Weren't you about to ask me something? I can stay if you need me to?" *Please say you need me to.*

Carson stepped closer and reached out, touching my hand briefly. He opened his mouth to say something, his eyes locked on mine, and I willed the words out of them, whatever they were.

I wanted to ask you if...

You'd go to the dance with me?

You'd go out with me?

Be my girlfriend?

I was *dying* to know.

But Ethan hovered in the entryway like a sentinel, rigid and unwavering. "I'm sure whatever it is can wait," he said. "Right, Carson?"

Carson closed his mouth and gave my hand

a little squeeze, offering me a smile, "Uh, yeah. Sure."

I deflated, hoping Ethan didn't notice my disappointment, but when I turned back toward the entryway to grab my coat, his eyes were on me. I avoided his gaze the entire time as I grabbed my jacket and slipped on my boots. It wasn't his fault I was disappointed. We got interrupted. Big deal. Carson and I could pick up where we left off. It's not like Ethan knew what I was feeling. I hadn't exactly been open with him about how I felt toward Carson.

It was an awkward thing—telling your best friend the boy you wanted was his brother.

I extended my box of Goobers toward Ethan once more, but he shook his head.

This wasn't how it worked with us.

He always ordered a large popcorn with extra butter, and I got the Goobers, while he pretended to hate them but ended up eating half the box. We usually switched snacks a quarter of the way through. But Ethan hadn't ordered anything except a soda, and so far, he hadn't so much as touched a Goober.

What the heck?

I sighed and turned my attention back to

the screen where the latest Marvel superhero movie played in all its HD digital glory. Ethan was a huge fan of these action flicks, and I never complained because occasionally he'd sit through one of my chick flicks. Besides, the men on these films had some serious muscles in their skintight costumes. All in all, it was worth the trade.

But today I wasn't into it. I kept getting lost in my thoughts, wondering why Ethan was so quiet. There were no jokes between us. No laughter when one of the characters did something super unrealistic or cheesy. No Ethan leaning toward me to explain what was happening because he intrinsically knew I was confused. No stealing my candy. Nothing.

It was excruciating.

By the time the credits rolled, I was more than ready for the movie to be over.

We headed back to Ethan's house in my car, and when I pulled up to the curb, instead of pulling into the driveway, he glanced at me like I had just punched him. "You're not coming up to hang out?"

I ran a hand through my hair, frustrated, and suddenly annoyed at him. "I don't know. Should I? You're not exactly talking to me. I figured you didn't want me around."

A moment passed before Ethan's gaze softened, and he was my best friend again. "Come on.

When do I *not* want to hang out?"

I debated a second before turning off the ignition and following him out of the car and into the house.

"You hungry?" he asked.

I shook my head. "I'll take some water, though."

Ethan headed for the kitchen and returned with a bottle of water. "Here." He handed it to me. "My mom says hello. She's working on the bills at the table, or she'd come out."

I cupped my hands around my mouth and hollered, "Hello, Mrs. Brooks."

"You wanna take these up?" Ethan asked, nodding toward the stairs.

"Sure."

I followed Ethan up to his bedroom, where I took a seat on the edge of his bed, cross-legged. He flopped down next to me, and the awkward silence that plagued us all evening came back.

I could see the glazed-over expression he'd had all evening returning, and I couldn't take it anymore. Something was up, and I wanted to know what. "What's going on?"

Ethan wouldn't meet my eyes. "What do you mean?"

"Are you serious, Ethan?" I paused, waiting

to see if he'd help me out. When he didn't, I hesitated before I took a deep breath and plunged right into what I thought was the crux of the problem. "Are you really that mad at me for hanging out with Carson?"

His eyes slid to mine, the hazel turning amber under the soft light.

But he said nothing, which only annoyed me more. "Because if you are, that's seriously unfair. You've been spending time with Beth, and I'm not all bent out of shape about it."

"That's different," he said.

My mouth dropped. *Seriously?* "How so?"

"Because I like her. You've always hated Carson and now all of a sudden you guys are best buds?"

Best buds? My thoughts drifted to our kiss, and I averted my gaze, unsure of how to respond because the way I felt about Carson had grown. It was big, beyond friendship, beyond anything I had ever felt before. My heart didn't race when I saw Ethan like it did around Carson. A flock of butterflies didn't threaten to riot when Ethan looked into my eyes. And my skin didn't tingle when he touched me. Not like it did with his brother.

"We're working on the Angel Program," I said in a feeble voice. It was a crap excuse, and I knew it. Luigi's, his meet, lunch, even hanging out the nights we organized the supplies, both ignoring the fact that we had been dragging it out for days, were far beyond the scope of the Angel Program.

"Okay." Ethan scoffed, his tone bitter. "The least you could do is be straight with me."

Frustrated, I curled my nails into my palms. "Why does it matter, anyway? We've always had other friends. We've dated, too. Why does my spending time with someone else matter now?"

"Because, Mia, isn't it obvious? He's my brother. Mr. Life of the Party, swim-star. You guys always hated each other. And you were always the one thing he wanted that was mine."

I flinched, and my stomach crumpled in on itself. "So you've been friends with me this whole time because I hated Carson? Because I was something he couldn't have?" I shook my head, trying to understand. "What're you even saying?"

"No, course not." Ethan stood and started to pace, kicking a dirty pair off gym shorts on his bedroom floor before he turned toward me. He closed his eyes and exhaled, then opened them again, staring into my eyes. "It's just. I always liked that it was you and me, ya know? I mean, sure, we have other friends. We've dated, but. . .I don't know. Everything feels like it's changing now."

"It is. We're older. I'll be going to school soon. But just because I realize Carson is different than I thought, that maybe he's not the bad guy I thought he was, doesn't mean things with us have to change. Aren't you the one all these years that's been telling me he wasn't so bad? To give him a chance?"

"Yeah, but I never thought you'd actually listen," he muttered. He reached up, clasping his hands behind his neck. "But now..."

"What?"

"You like him, right? Like, really like him." He searched my expression for the truth, his gaze earnest.

A part of me was afraid of what he'd see. "I...I don't know," I stammered.

But I did know. I absolutely knew. I was just afraid to admit it. For some reason, telling Ethan the truth felt like a betrayal.

"Mia..."

"Maybe?" I said like it was a question.

He swallowed, then glanced away for a moment. "It just feels weird. I've been hanging out with Beth more, and you're starting to like Carson. Both of you will be leaving at the end of the summer, and I'll still be here..." he trailed off, staring at something on the wall opposite him.

I let him process his thoughts because he was right. A lot was changing. If anyone knew that, it was me. All I had to do was spend an afternoon at home to realize just how much things had changed. And it frightened me too, but I couldn't just ignore it.

"I see the way he looks at you," Ethan muttered.

My head whipped toward him, my heart in my throat. "What do you mean?"

Ethan rolled his eyes. "Come on, Mia. It's not even the kiss on the cheek he purposely did to annoy me. It's the way he looks at you when you're not watching. Like you're the best thing in the room, the same way he's looked at you for years. He's liked you since the day you met at the beach. But you were always mine. *My* friend. Right from the start."

I swallowed. Hard. My mouth went dry. "I can be both," I said, leaving the insinuation hanging between us—*both Carson's girl and your best friend.*

"What if it's supposed to be us?"

I blinked. "Us?" A weird feeling shimmied down my spine.

Ethan nodded, his mouth set. His expression was more serious than I'd ever seen it. Reaching out, he slid a hand to the base of my neck, and I froze.

"Ethan...?"

"Have you ever thought about us being together? Before today I never really did, but when I saw you with Carson the other day, it made me think. You've been my best friend for nine years. All this time, you've been the one there for me. We've shared everything together. It's always been us. What if it's supposed to be us now?"

I wanted to shake my head, *No*, to talk some sense into him. But what happened next was so fast I couldn't stop it. He leaned forward and pressed his lips to mine.

CHAPTER FOURTEEN

Alarm bells blared in my head as Ethan's lips moved overtop of mine. They were warm and soft. But they felt all wrong. It was totally weird, like when you took a sip of your drink, expecting it to be something else entirely, and the surprise of it—the reality of it—hit you in a single instant of recognition and you cringe inside.

My palms made contact with his chest, ready to shove him off of me when he pulled away.

A thud outside his door drew our attention, momentarily saving us from post-kiss awkwardness. And when I glanced to the sound, his door swung softly on its hinge, like someone had nudged it open. I swore I saw movement in the hall, so I got up and ran to check, but found it empty.

The house was eerily quiet as I turned back to him. "Um. . ." I started, stupidly, because how did you tell your best friend in the whole world that kissing him was like kissing a paper sack?

"Ugh. That was gross," Ethan blurted. He grimaced and furiously wiped at his mouth. "You kiss like my grandma."

A giggle escaped my lips, and I had to slap a hand over my mouth to prevent full-on hysteria because the relief I felt was so monumental. "Seriously? My hand kisses better than you."

Ethan pulled a face. "Doubtful, but what was I thinking?"

"You tell me."

Ethan grinned, looking sheepish. "Sorry."

"Did you get that out of your system?"

"*Totally*. Please forget I ever said anything. I was *so* wrong."

"Thank heavens."

We laughed, and then it grew silent again.

Ethan picked at a loose thread on his bedspread when he said, "Sorry. I think I was just jealous when I saw you and Carson together. Not because I like you. That kiss cleared that up." He shuddered, and I whipped his pillow off the bed and threw it at his face. After he caught it, he laughed and added, "We haven't been hanging as much, and I'm dreading you leaving next year. I guess when I saw you guys getting along, I freaked. Call it temporary insanity."

I shook my head. "You're such an idiot, but I'm sure Beth will be relieved because I think she really likes you, and you two will be super cute together if you'd get your crap together and finally, officially, ask her out to more than just the dance."

He widened his eyes comically. "After that kiss, I am."

"Ha, ha. Just don't try that again," I said, motioning between us. "Ever. Or you'll be one ball short."

Ethan cupped his crotch. "No worries."

"Did Carson ask you yet?"

"To the dance?" I asked.

He nodded.

I glanced down to my hands. "Not yet."

As if reading my thoughts, Ethan stood and squeezed my shoulder. "He will." Then he headed for the hall.

"Hey, where are you going?" I asked. Now that we returned to normal, he was leaving?

"To Lysol my mouth. Be right back."

I grabbed the pillow again and threw it, but

he jumped out of the way, and his laughter rang out, down the hallway.

Up until this point, the Angel Program had been a breeze. But today, not so much.

Carson and I had gotten along so well. But somehow, in the last three days, we went from like to hate—kissing to the silent treatment.

It started with him standing me up yesterday morning. We were supposed to meet with Mrs. Parks in the afternoon, after Carson's practice, but he never showed. He never even answered my texts until later that evening, and even then, his response was the equivalent of a virtual shrug.

He forgot—his exact words.

Lucky for him, I covered for him and told her that his swim meet ran late. It was risky. Mrs. Parks could've easily made her way to the high school pool to see if the team was still there, but she didn't question it. Instead, she was just thrilled to have the boxes filled with the Angel Tree gifts all accounted for, wrapped, and with my help, piled inside of her car. I updated her on the adopted families and assured her that we had all presents packaged and ready to go. All we needed was to shop for groceries, divvy them up, then deliver everything.

But as I waited for him that afternoon at the Sweet Water Market, impatiently checking my time on the phone, I realized that he wasn't going to show.

Sick of waiting, I sent him a disgusted text and did the grocery shopping myself. Instead of enjoying it like I had when we went shopping together for the gifts, I hated every single solitary minute. I had to somehow navigate two carts, then park them to go and grab a third. By the time I was done, I was exhausted and made a point to call Ethan to ensure Carson wasn't home. The last thing I wanted was to see him at the moment. I didn't want a confrontation and couldn't trust myself not to say something stupid.

When I pulled into the driveway, Ethan was already waiting for me. He helped me unload everything into the house, which we divided among the boxes. Luckily, Mrs. Brooks had made room in her refrigerator for the cold items like the deli trays and Christmas hams.

The entire time we worked, Ethan continued flicking worried looks my way, which I tried studiously to ignore.

"This is ridiculous. He should be here," Ethan said.

"No kidding." It was all I could think of to say.

He shook his head. "It doesn't make sense.

He helped you this whole time. To just stop now is weird. I heard Mom talking to him this morning, too. She asked him if he was supposed to help you today and he said you didn't need his help. That you'd handled it. Handled it, my a—"

"It's fine." I snapped, then sighed. "I'm sorry. I just don't want to talk about it, okay? You're here now, and I'm sure he'll be here tonight to help deliver. We're supposed to use his Jeep."

"But I thought you two were getting along? What happened?"

"Your guess is as good as mine," I said through gritted teeth.

When we placed the final bag in the freezer, Ethan turned to me. "Hey, Beth and I are supposed to go out tonight, but you and I can catch lunch if you want?"

I shook my head and tried for a small smile. "Nah. I'm tired. I'll just go home until later when we're supposed to deliver everything, then I'll be back."

"Okay. But call if you want company."

"Will do," I said, even though I had no intentions of doing so. The only thing I wanted was to wallow away in my bedroom.

CHAPTER FIFTEEN

T he minute I got home, my day went from bad to worse.

The living room was a war zone. Clothes were strewn everywhere, along with what appeared to be a set of bed sheets, and what I recognized as my father's luggage. In the middle of the mess was the Christmas tree, lying haphazardly, half out of the box, along with the plastic bins of ornaments, like my mom had decided to put it up after all, then gave up.

Shouting came from the master bedroom down the hall, and it didn't take a genius to figure out what happened—clearly, my parents had gotten into some kind of epic fight. 'Tis the season.

I sighed as I picked my way through the living room, heading to the kitchen for a glass of water when my gaze landed on a pile of mail on the kitchen table.

Something pulled at me, urged me over. I reached out and grabbed the envelope on top with shaking hands. Sure enough, University of North Carolina Chapel Hill was printed in the left-hand corner in bold letters.

I squeezed my eyes closed, and my parents shouting faded to the background as I said a little prayer, then tore it open. With shaking hands, I pulled out the letter inside. And my heart dropped.

Dear Miss Mia Randalls,

We at the University of North Carolina at Chapel Hill regret to inform you...

I dropped my hands, and my vision blurred with tears. I didn't need to read the rest of the letter to know what it said. Those opening words were enough.

We regret to inform you...

We regret to inform you...

Five tiny words that were like a knife in my back.

I didn't get in. And while UNC wasn't my first choice, I had yet to hear from Duke or any of the other colleges. Early admission was reserved for the exceptional, I told myself. For people with talent like Carson. Not for people like me.

I ground my teeth as I tore the letter to shreds, then threw the remnants in the air, watching them flutter around me like confetti. When the sound of footsteps grew closer, I broke free from my pity party to listen as they stopped, just outside the kitchen.

My parents probably hadn't realized I came home yet, I mused. I should tell them. It was the right thing to do, so they didn't say something they didn't want me to hear. But I couldn't seem to move my feet. I couldn't seem to care.

Then my father's voice burst through the walls and the knife twisted a little deeper. "I am so sick of this. Sick of everything. It's the same old crap," he yelled.

I flinched, as though he said those words to me and not my mom.

"No one's forcing you to stay, Dan," Mom shouted, her voice cutting like a knife. "You can leave at any time."

"Fine," Dad barked. "I want a divorce."

His voice cut, blade sharp. Everything went silent.

I had expected it. Hadn't I? I had anticipated this moment for a long time, almost hoped for it these past months because I couldn't take one more second of the fighting. But now it was here, and I wished it away.

The answering silence was deafening. All I wanted to do was erase the last ten seconds, wipe it from my brain. I wanted the fighting back, the screaming matches, and the finger-pointing. As awful as those things were, at least they meant I had both of my parents. Because all that would remain once those things were gone was. . .nothing —silence. Suddenly, I wasn't so sure which would be worse.

Two days before Christmas and my parents wanted a divorce. The thought crushed me, made my insides twist with dread.

With purpose, I slowly walked into the living room on wooden legs. When I entered, I saw my parents, standing face-to-face, limbs trembling with anger, faces contorted in rage, and a pain so deep it made my throat ache. It took them a whole minute to realize I was standing there.

I wanted to shout, to yell like they'd been yelling, *Remember me, your daughter? I live here. I'm part of this family, too.* But the moment Dad's gaze turned to mine, his eyes widened in shock first, then shame, and Mom's mask crumpled as she cried.

And I remembered that no matter how badly this hurt, it wasn't about me. Not everything was about me, and I couldn't save them. Not with good behavior, straight As, or early admission to Duke. My parents' relationship had been over a long time ago. It just took them this long to admit it. Nothing I could say would change that.

"Mia," my mother hurried forward, her hands fluttering out in front of her in the way they often did when she was upset or nervous.

I took a step back, holding a hand out like a linebacker's stiff-arm. Luckily, she got the hint and backed off.

Mom cleared her throat. "Honey, we need to talk."

"Do you think I'm deaf? Or blind? Like I can't see what's happening? Like I think all of this is normal?" I asked, waving madly around the room.

"Mia. . ." Dad tried to grab my arm, but I wrenched it away and sidestepped him.

"I told you this was affecting her," my mother said, her eyes blazing as she stared at my father, accusation oozing from her pores.

"Oh, and I suppose it's all my fault?" he snapped.

"Well, it sure ain't all mine," Mom shouted.

Oh. My. Gosh.

I growled as I shoved my hands into my hair, yanking slightly at the roots, needing the slight discomfort as a reminder that I was, in fact, alive and standing in the living room with them. I was there—flesh and blood—they were just so blinded by their own anger to see me.

I squeezed my eyes closed as their bickering escalated, before I snapped, "Stop! For the love of all that's holy. Just. Stop."

The room fell silent. No denial, no arguments. Just silence.

Mom's stunned expression at my outburst morphed into one of mortification. I never raised my voice to them, never lost my cool. They were so used to me being the "perfect" daughter. I did everything right to the point of exhaustion. The day I tried to choke Carson was probably the only time in my life I could remember doing anything worth punishing.

I didn't wait for an answer or a response. Instead, I bounded up the stairs, letting the thudding sound of my footsteps be my closing argument, retreating into the haven of my room. Only a couple minutes later, I was antsy. I couldn't sit still, and the knot in the back of my throat moved to my heart when my gaze landed on the mini Christmas tree lit up on my desk.

My stomach wrenched. Why wasn't Carson responding to my texts or calling me back? Why'd he stand me up? Not once, but twice.

I flopped onto my bed and laid there, staring

at the little plastic bulbs hanging from the artificial pine. I finally got my wish for silence, and now that I had it, it was ominous—the resounding death knell of my parent's marriage and our life together as a family.

Unable to take it any longer, I got up, grabbed my phone and jacket, and headed for my car. I drove to the beach and parked in one of the public beach access parking lots. In the summer, these spots were like gold, but in late December, there wasn't a car in sight.

I made my way up the old, wooden planked path, over the giant dunes, and toward the beach. The sound of the waves greeted me before the sight of the vast blue. But once I crested the stairs, the dark waters greeted me. Foamy whitecaps crashed to shore in a familiar and soothing cadence, and I knew from experience the dark waters would be cold as ice.

I watched for a moment, pushing my thoughts aside and letting the ocean soothe me before I descended the stairs and made my way toward the shoreline, my Converse chucks sinking into the damp sand the whole way.

I stood until the toes of my shoes were just far enough away from the water's edge, not to risk getting soaked. I don't know how long I stared out into the horizon before the dam on my thoughts broke, but once it did, everything came crashing in like a high tide.

My parent's marriage was over.

I got rejected from UNC.

I still haven't heard from Duke, but it was probably a "no."

Carson was avoiding me.

Soon, high school would be over, and where would I be?

All these things and more flooded my brain.

Not having any answers scared me, maybe more than anything. But one thing was clear. Nothing would ever be the same again.

After some time, I turned and made my way up the beach, then realized with a start that I wasn't alone. Sometime during my mini breakdown, a small group of people had started a bonfire.

I watched as several guys lugged coolers onto the beach, and they began collecting driftwood for a fire. Then two girls ran down the dunes, and I recognized them—Tasha and Olivia. Not exactly the people I felt like running into.

The familiar peel of Olivia's laughter drifted toward me, a warning that if I didn't want to be seen, I'd better hurry and get off the beach while they were distracted with setting up what was clearly going to be a small beach party. But it was too late because her eyes locked on mine just as I started for the stairs.

"Guys, it's Mia," Olivia announced.

I froze, sighing inwardly as I glanced over at them with a smile and a half-hearted wave.

When she called me over, I hesitated, but ultimately, I went because it wasn't like I could ignore them. Turning back, I trudged through the sand toward them and came to a stop in front of Olivia, who looked far better in a baggy hoodie and skinny jeans than anyone had a right to.

"Hey, having a party?" I asked, hoping I could make a minute of small talk and then bail.

"Yeah," Olivia said. "Wanna stay a minute and hang?"

"I can't," I said, more grateful than ever I had a convenient excuse to leave. I hooked a thumb back toward the walkway. "I've got to deliver the packages for the Angel Program. I'm actually meeting Carson in a few minutes, so I have to get going."

"Carson?" Olivia scrunched her nose, and I wanted to tell her it was unattractive

"Yeah. Remember? It was our remediation project."

"No, I know that, but it's just. . ." She

grinned, and something vicious glinted in her eye —sharp and lethal—a warning for me to brace myself. "I ran into Carson this morning. He was at the pool swimming, and I saw him in the lot on his way out. We went to lunch, and then I invited him to the party. He said he'd come." Olivia shrugged and reached out, placing a hand on my arm, her smile saccharine. "Looks like you'll be delivering packages alone."

So, that's where he was this morning. When he was supposed to be grocery shopping with me for the Angel families, he was out with Olivia. Nice. I wonder where he was yesterday when I met with Mrs. Parks too.

I fisted my hands at my side, letting the information wash over me. "I'm sure he'll be there. He probably just meant he was stopping by after," I said, trying to save face. "He wouldn't do that to me—leave me to everything alone."

Olivia gasped theatrically, covering her mouth with one hand, then reached out again to squeeze my arm. "Oh, honey. That's so sweet. You think he cares about you, don't you?"

I clenched my teeth, saying nothing.

"I'm sorry, but maybe you shouldn't reach quite so high, you know. I'm your friend, so I want to be real with you. You're nice, and cute and all, but guys like Carson, they go out with girls like me. I'd hate to see you get hurt. Just try to stay in

225

your lane, hun."

I glanced away, biting my tongue, and struggling to conjure a smile, to put on a brave face. The best thing I could do was thank her for the advice like I normally would, then move on. It was simpler that way. But I was tired of swallowing down my emotions, tired of easy, and sick of getting steamrolled. Maybe self-restraint was overrated.

"You know, Olivia, for someone so pretty, you're so ugly when you open your mouth." I smiled one of her trademark plastic smiles—equal parts malicious and disingenuous—then ripped her hand off my arm.

Olivia's eyes widened, and her face turned red. Clearly, she wasn't used to people telling her off.

But it felt oh-so-good. I made her angry. Or embarrassed her. Or both.

But I wasn't done yet. I had years of pent-up aggression, waiting for me to give it a voice.

I stepped forward and poked her in the chest. "You know what I think? I think Carson turned you down." I had no idea if that was the case. He probably hadn't, and I was an idiot for saying it, but something deep down told me it was true. Olivia and Tasha always seemed to get what they wanted, but I had seen the way Carson looked at her at The Bean and then at his party. Like it was a chore just being around her.

"That's ridiculous." She flipped her bleached-out hair over her shoulder, but she wouldn't meet my eye.

"Is it? Because you all but told him you wanted him to ask you to the Snowflake Ball, but he didn't, did he?"

Her mouth opened and closed like a beached Flounder in the most satisfying way.

"That's what I thought," I said and figured if I wanted to make my exit, this was as good a time as any.

I turned my back to her and started up the dunes toward the walkway when she called out behind me, "You can't just talk to me like that!"

When I said nothing, she continued, "I didn't want to go to the stupid dance with him anyway!" Then I heard her and Tasha conversing, the word "loser" sprinkled in their conversation, but I didn't care because my feet were hitting the wooden planks in a steady cadence, shoulders back, head lifted high. I told my parents what I thought. I stood up to Olivia. And it felt good.

CHAPTER SIXTEEN

T he adrenaline from my encounter with Olivia was short-lived.

I stood in the chilly air, waiting outside the Brooks' home, with no sign of Carson in sight.

The thought crossed my mind that Olivia had been telling the truth. Maybe he was on his way to the beach that very second.

Talk about eating crow.

No, I told myself. I couldn't think like that. Even if Carson did stand me up and go to the party on the beach, it didn't negate the things I said to Olivia. They were still true. For the most part.

When I rang the doorbell one last time

and no one answered, I called Ethan. Pressing the phone to my ear, I sighed in relief at the sound of his voice. "'Sup, my lady friend?"

"You out with Beth?"

"Yeah, why? What's up?"

I sighed. "I guess you don't know where your brother is, do you?" I asked.

"Oh, man. He's not home?" Ethan asked in a gentle voice.

"If he were home, would I be standing outside your house in the cold waiting on him?"

"Okay, I sense you're on the verge of a breakdown. So, deep breath," he said, inhaling and exhaling loudly into the phone.

"Ethan!" I stomped my foot even though there was no one to see.

"Okay, okay. Just trying to help, but I thought he was home before I left. If you need help, Beth and I could come for a bit. Just say the word, and we're there."

Ugh. That's all I needed was to be a third wheel right now.

"No. I'm fine, but all the stuff is in your house. I can put everything in my car, but I still need inside to get everything."

"Say no more. I'll text you the code to get in."

"Thanks," I said, wishing I felt more relief. But, really, I hated doing this alone. I hated that Carson hadn't shown. He was probably at the beach right now, flirting with Olivia.

"And Mia?"

I startled, thinking he had already hung up. "Yeah?"

"I don't care if he is my brother, I'm kicking his a—"

"Thanks, Ethan," I said, cutting him off.

I hung up and waited as the text came through. Once I punched in the code to the keypad on the side door, I went inside and surveyed the living room. All the boxes Carson and I had packed together were still scattered throughout.

I made my way toward one and traced my finger over Carson's sloppy handwriting, and it all hit me. My parents. Carson. Even my confrontation with Olivia stirred a painful ache inside my chest I couldn't squelch, and the tears I had suppressed all day rose to the surface. Being dateless for the Snowflake Ball was the least of my worries.

I crouched in front of the boxes labeled "Adams Family" and reached for the first one as a tear slid down my cheek. Wiping it away, I stood, balancing the heavy box in front of me when the front door slammed.

I turned around, expecting to see Ethan. He

had come after all.

"That was fast..." My words trailed off, lost in the lump in my throat. Because it wasn't Ethan. It was Carson.

His dark hair was more rumpled than usual, and his cheeks slightly flushed from the cold. He moved closer, coming to stand in front of me. Something about the way he held himself, the way he couldn't seem to meet my eyes told me he was nervous.

He reached up and tugged on the drawstrings of his hoodie, looking more adorable than was fair.

"You came," I said.

"Here, let me get that." He reached for the box, then set it on the ground next to him. Once he stood back up, he shoved his hands in the pockets of his Wild Cat joggers and stared at me. "Were you crying?" he asked, his voice gruff as he reached out and brushed a thumb over my damp cheek.

"You didn't show yesterday with Mrs. Parks, then today at Sweet Water Market—"

"I know. I'm sorry, but I..." He paused, glancing to the side as if working something out in his head before turning his blue eyes back to mine. "Do you like my brother, Mia?"

"Of course I like your brother."

"No." He shook his head. "Do you *like* him

like him?"

"What? No." I crossed my arms over my chest, a wave of irritation flushing my face.

"Because I thought you and me..." He huffed like speaking was difficult, then growled and raked his hands through his hair, then muttered, "Why is this so hard?"

The heat of my anger thawed as I took in his expression. He seemed almost desperate when he asked, "Then why'd you kiss him?"

I frowned. "Why'd I..." It took me a second to understand. "What?" I whispered, and all the air rushed from my lungs. It all made sense. He saw us—the thudding noise outside of Ethan's room must've been him. I could've sworn I had seen someone.

"You kissed him. I saw you guys," he said, confirming my worst fears. "I came to see you, and I went to his room to see if you wanted to hang out, and I saw you kissing."

My palms dampened and sweat pricked my back. Of course Carson chose that exact moment —a moment that lasted two seconds—to peek inside Ethan's room. So, this is why he didn't show yesterday or this morning. This is why he gave me the cold shoulder and answered none of my calls.

I would've done the same.

How did I explain this without sounding

like a total liar?

Stepping forward, I pleaded, "I realize how bad that must've looked, but—"

"Do you?" he snapped.

I dropped my arms, surprised by his tone and the anger churning in his eyes. He could at least let me explain. And then I remembered what Olivia told me.

"I don't know why it matters, anyway. Not when you're ditching me to spend time with Olivia. Tell me. . .when you were supposed to meet Mrs. Parks with me, and then this morning when you were supposed to meet me at the market, where were you? Did you and Olivia have fun laughing at me this morning? *Oh, poor, little Mia, getting stood up.* How funny."

His eyes widened, giving himself away, but I wasn't done. The tears came back, stinging my eyes with a vengeance. "So why do you care what I do, when you so clearly do whatever you want?"

He gripped my arms in his hands and yelled, "Because you matter to me. Don't you get it?"

I swallowed.

Silence consumed the air around us. *I mattered to him.*

"You've always mattered. All these years, the stupid fights, the teasing. . .It was all just a way to get to you." Carson drew in a shaky breath, then turned around and shoved his hands in his hair, pacing before he pivoted back around to face me. "I thought we had something; you know? I thought"—he shook his head—"I don't know, like, we were working toward something, and then I go in his room, and I see *that,* and I—"

"It was a mistake," I said, hoping he'd listen. "For the record, Ethan kissed me. I didn't even kiss him back, and though I admit I was in shock for a second, I pushed him away the moment I even realized what had happened. And it was awful. Like really, *really* awful." I grimaced.

I could only imagine what Ethan would say if he heard me, but it was the truth, and I had to make Carson believe me. "It was like kissing my grandfather," I said, stealing Ethan's words.

I was totally blowing this. If I were Carson, I would never believe me, which meant whatever we had was over. All because of that single moment Ethan decided to become jealous.

I was going to throttle him.

I brought my fingers to my temples, panic swelling in my chest. "He apologized afterward and said he was just freaked out because he got jealous of the time we were spending together and how everything was changing. I have *never* liked Ethan in that way. Not in the nine years I've known him. He has always been just a friend to me. I like *you*." Then in a softer voice, I mustered my courage and said, "You're the one I want."

His eyes locked on mine.

"I know it's crazy," I said. "I mean, me and Carson Brooks? Who would've thought, but I—" His mouth crushed mine, and I had never been more grateful to not have to finish a sentence.

He kissed me dizzy. Kissed away my words, all my fears. And when he pulled away, his gaze flickered over my face, assessing. "How was that?"

I exhaled. "I'm not sure." He frowned in response, and I added, "You better kiss me again. Just to be sure."

Then he grinned and kissed me again.

EPILOGUE

I smoothed the bodice of my royal-blue velvet dress and smiled. It was a miracle I found one on such short notice, but not only did I find a gown, I found one I loved. It was gorgeous with long, sheer sleeves and a sweetheart neckline. It fit my curves like a glove, and when I walked, the slit gave a peek of my legs and sky-high silver heels.

My prince paused when he saw me step outside. Based on the slight widening of his eyes and the hitch in his step, I knew I chose well, and I counted off my list of accomplishments in my head.

Carson mesmerized.

My very own Prince Charming carrying a bouquet of red roses.

A date with the most handsome guy at Sweet Water.

My gaze flickered over his perfectly tailored navy-blue suit and silver tie. His dark hair had been tamed into a stylishly messy quaff, and his blue eyes glittered—brighter than any ocean I've ever seen.

Carson resumed his way up the walkway, his eyes fixed on my face. I smiled at him, and when he finally reached me, he handed me the flowers, then placed a hand on his chest, over his heart and grinned. He shook his head and laughed a little before he leaned in and whispered, "You're so beautiful, I'm speechless."

When he pulled away, it took everything in me not to throw myself at him and kiss the smile off his face, but my parents were watching, so I maintained my dignity—just barely—and said, "Carson Brooks speechless? That's a first."

Smirking, he raised a brow. "Ready?"

When he reached out, offering me his arm, I nodded, turning briefly to my parents. They stood on either side of me. My father had moved out three days ago—the day after Christmas. It would take me a while to adjust to this new dynamic, but for tonight, I was focusing on the dance, on Carson, on my future.

I handed my mom the flowers and asked her to put them in water for me, then waved goodbye to them, and hooked my arm in Carson's, allowing him to escort me to his Jeep. Leaning against the side of it were Ethan and Beth, both dressed in black.

I smiled at him as we drew near. In the end, he had been right. We *both* had dates to the Snowflake Ball. My life may still be a mess, but for once, I wasn't trying to control everything, and I no longer cared what people thought about me. If the last few weeks had taught me anything, it was to live in the moment and enjoy the ride. I couldn't take responsibility for everything, only my own happiness. In the end, things would be okay. I would be okay.

When we stopped in front of Carson's Jeep, Ethan offered his brother a head nod, then turned his smile to me. "Told you we'd find you a date."

I laughed, thinking about the day in the gymnasium when I snapped and tried to strangle Carson.

"What's so funny?" Carson asked.

"I can't believe we're together."

"Me neither, especially after I left that welt on your eye with the basketball. You should've seen your face." He laughed, and I smacked him lightly on the chest.

"I saw yours," I shot back. "When I tried to unsuccessfully throttle you."

Ethan snorted. "Just think, had Mr. Gorby not pulled you off him, we wouldn't be here right now."

We all laughed, and I added, "Who would've thought I'd end up with the boy who tried to drown me when I was nine?"

Carson opened my door, then rounded the other side. "Hey, I was a kid. It was my way of flirting."

He closed his door, and I reached across the seat to grab his tie. I tugged on it, pulling him closer, murmuring against his mouth, "Thank, goodness, your flirting skills have improved over the years, huh?" Then I pressed my mouth to his, sinking into the kiss until Ethan groaned behind us and started banging on the backs of our seats.

"Come on, guys," he said. "You promised you'd keep the PDAs to a minimum tonight."

"We're not even in public yet," Carson protested.

"There are two other people in this car, so it counts as public domain."

When Carson grumbled, I laughed. He turned the keys in the ignition and started the engine. "Wait!" I screamed.

Carson jerked in his seat. "What?"

"You just about gave me a heart attack," Ethan whined.

"I almost forgot," I said, then reaching into my clutch, I pulled out the envelope and pushed it toward him. "Read it."

His brows furrowed as he turned his questioning gaze from me to the envelope. I watched as he paused, reading the return address, waiting for it to register. His eyes lit up before he tore into it, yanked the letter out, unfolded it, and read out loud, "We at Duke University, are pleased to grant you, Mia Randalls, early admission into the..." His voice trailed off before he flung the letter aside and lunged at me, crushing his mouth over mine again as I laughed.

By the time he pulled away, I was breathless, and it took me a moment to clear my head. "Looks like we'll be going to school together in the fall. Think you can handle that, Brooks?"

He smirked. "The real question is, do you think Durham can handle that? Carson Brooks and his girlfriend, Mia Randalls. Watch out Duke, here we come."

A swarm of butterflies rioted in my stomach. It was the first time he referred to me as his girlfriend. Slowly this time, I closed the distance, but before my lips could meet his, Ethan leaned past the front seats between us. "If I have to watch my best friend and my brother make out one more time, I'll vomit all over this precious Jeep."

"You're such a killjoy," Carson said.

But all I could do was smile, sighing contentedly as we pulled away from the curb and headed for the Sweet Water gymnasium. My life may still be messy, and parts of my future uncertain, but already, things were looking up.

ABOUT THE AUTHOR

Tia Souders is a city girl turned country. If life on a farm isn't interesting enough, renovating a century home with her hubs has kept her on her toes. There's nothing like discovering a fried squirrel in your furnace to make life fresh again.

She's an unapologetic wine-loving, coffeeholic with a sweet tooth. In-between wrangling her two children and drinking copious amounts of coffee, she reads and writes stories that tug on your heartstrings.

Visit her at tiasouders.com and join her newsletter for sneak peeks and more!